"The press is still here. Is that what you wanted?"

Philipa turned to Bart for confirmation and caught her breath. He wasn't looking at the heavy piece of equipment, he was looking at her, and there was an unnerving hunger in his blue eyes.

"It wasn't all I wanted," he said softly.

She could feel her eyes widening. And she knew she only had to smile at him, to move closer....

He put both his hands on her shoulders, but he didn't attempt to draw her against him. He said, "I haven't given up, Philipa. I still think our partnership shouldn't be limited to office hours. I've thought about it a lot while I've been away." His voice deepened. "I want you very much. I don't seem to be able to get you out of my system."

Marjorie Lewty is a born romantic. "It's all in the way you look at the world," she suggests. "Maybe if I hadn't been lucky enough to find love myself—in my parents, my husband, my children—I might have viewed the world with cynicism." As it is, she writes about "what is surely the most important and exciting part of growing up, and that is falling in love." She and her family live in Leamington, a pleasant town full of beautiful parks and old Georgian homes.

THE BEGINNING OF THE AFFAIR
Marjorie Lewty

Harlequin Books

TORONTO • NEW YORK • LONDON
AMSTERDAM • PARIS • SYDNEY • HAMBURG
STOCKHOLM • ATHENS • TOKYO • MILAN
MADRID • WARSAW • BUDAPEST • AUCKLAND

Original hardcover edition published in 1992
by Mills & Boon Limited

ISBN 0-373-17130-7

Harlequin Romance first edition March 1993

THE BEGINNING OF THE AFFAIR

CHAPTER ONE

ON THE afternoon of Father's funeral Philippa decided that the day had arrived for a new self-image. For the first time in her twenty-one years she was free to please herself, and that was exactly what she intended to do.

'No, Robert,' she heard herself saying, rather to her own surprise. 'It's kind of you to offer, but no.'

Philippa, her elder brother Robert and her elder sister Chloe were in the first-floor living-room of the immensely tall Regency house in the Warwickshire spa town. Ethel, Robert's wife, had cried off coming to the funeral when the baby-sitter had failed to turn up to look after the twins.

Robert, twelve years Philippa's senior, was standing with his back to the small fire that was doing its best to take the January chill off the high, draughty room. Robert was every inch the successful executive, long legs in their expensively tailored charcoal trousers planted firmly a little apart on the red Turkey carpet, fair hair slicked back, large, handsome face serious, as befitted the occasion. And Robert went on laying down the law, just as Father might have done, as if Philippa hadn't spoken.

'We'll put this house on the market as soon as possible. You needn't bother your head about that, I'll arrange it all for you, and meanwhile you'll come back to Solihull with Ethel and me, of course. You can't stay here alone. Then we'll have to see what can be done about getting rid of the business.'

He cleared his throat importantly and went on, 'It won't be easy to sell, I'm afraid. Father's printing venture can hardly be classed as a ''going concern'' at the moment, and——' he shook his head '—the house needs a good deal of renovation and repair. Still, you never know, someone might be interested in buying a printing firm and a house to go with it.'

'No,' Philippa said again, and saying it was easier the second time. She edged forward on the heavy crimson velvet sofa, sitting up very straight and planting her size four shoes firmly on the floor. She was wearing a grey jersey dress with a deep white collar, which emphasised her delicate slenderness. But her small, rather beautiful face, with its huge smoky grey eyes and softly vulnerable mouth, framed by her silky fall of near-black hair, took on an unaccustomed look of determination. 'Thank you very much, Robert, but I'd rather stay here for the time being. We have several orders to work through in the printing shop, which means that there's the office work to be attended to. And,' she added with a firmness that even Robert couldn't ignore, 'I don't propose to sell the house, or the printing business. I mean to carry on just as we are.'

There was a faint chuckle from the opposite sofa, where Chloe, taking time off from her top PA job in Paris to attend the funeral, sat back, elegant in her black, fine-wool designer suit, displaying a good deal of her long, sleek legs, a smile of amusement quirking her perfectly painted mouth.

Robert ignored her. He and Chloe didn't get on at all well these days. His pale blue eyes, so like Father's, goggled at Philippa. 'Carry on—alone? But you can't possibly.'

'I can try,' Philippa said.

'Hear, hear,' put in Chloe amusedly.

Robert came and sat beside Philippa on the sofa. 'Funny, gallant little Pippa,' he said, taking her hand in his and patting it with tolerant affection.

Philippa withdrew her hand. 'I'm not a child, Robert,' she said quietly.

Robert's fair brows lifted at this unaccustomed sign of mutiny. He said kindly, 'You're tired out, Pippa. Looking after Father as well as keeping the office going has been a terrible strain for you. I only wish we could have helped more, but of course Ethel's health hasn't been too good since the twins were born. But now it's all over you need a good long rest. You really must let us take care of you for a while. Ethel will be delighted, and you can help with the children if you feel inclined. I'll see that things are looked after here. I'll send someone along from my office to keep an eye on the books.'

'It's good of you to offer,' Philippa said, thinking that 'helping' with Robert's obstreperous two-year-old twin boys wasn't likely to be much of a rest, 'but I've quite made up my mind. I shall stay here.'

Robert frowned. 'I don't like it. I don't like it at all. It's my business as head of the family now to see that you're properly situated.'

Chloe giggled. 'Don't be so pompous, Robert.'

Robert glared at her, bristling, as Philippa said quite gently, deliberately misunderstanding, 'Well, actually, it's *my* business, isn't it?' She was pleased that her voice sounded so steady. 'Father left it to me in his will, together with the house.'

'Yes, yes, of course.' Robert could barely conceal his impatience. 'Father and I decided some time ago that that was the best way to be sure you would be provided for, being so much younger than Chloe and me.'

'Well, then,' she said quite firmly. 'I *am* provided for. I have a house and a business, so you really don't need to worry about me.'

Robert waved that away. 'You don't understand, Pippa. Father and I agreed that I, as executor, would take care of everything on your behalf should any-thing—er—unforeseen happen to him.'

'Just as Father always took care of everything for me when he was alive,' Philippa said drily.

'Precisely,' said Robert. He frowned slightly, turning a reproving eye on her.

She saw his lips compress and, anticipating a lecture, went on quickly, 'But that's beside the point. The point is that I appreciate your offer of help, Robert, and I'm sure you mean it kindly, but I'm twenty-one now—twenty-two in October—and I think it's time I took my life in my own hands. I've been working here with Father for over three years, and I believe I know all there is to know about the business side of the firm.'

'Yes, yes, I'm sure you do,' Robert humoured her. 'You're a clever girl. But knowing about it and having all the responsibility on your shoulders are two different things.'

'I think responsibility is what I need,' Philippa said.

Robert took refuge in jocularity. 'Well, my offer of help remains on the table. I won't put any pressure on you, Pippa. You must go ahead and see what you can do on your own without Big Brother looking over your shoulder.'

'I will,' she said cheerfully. 'And I'll get in touch with the solicitors when I need some money.'

He laughed indulgently. 'I can see you're going to make a real little businesswoman.' His face sobered as he added, 'But I'm afraid the coffers will be almost empty once the funeral expenses are paid. I'm seeing the solicitor next week myself, but I'm not very optimistic. Now, be a good girl and do as I say. Let me help you.' He produced what he must have thought was a winning smile as he got to his feet and took his overcoat from the back of the sofa.

Philippa got up too, standing very straight, making the most of her five feet four inches as her brother towered above her.

'Don't patronise me, Robert,' she said. And then, 'Are you sure you wouldn't like another cup of tea before you go?'

Five minutes later Philippa and Chloe stood on the front step and waved their brother goodbye as he drove off to his Solihull home.

'That's that.' Philippa closed the heavy front door. She sighed. The house seemed odd without Father; she would miss his autocratic presence, his endless demands on her time and patience. 'Let's go up to my flat,' she said. 'The family rooms give me the creeps, now Father's gone.'

'They always gave me the creeps.' Chloe shivered delicately, following Philippa up the stairs to the second floor. 'All that hideous, heavy furniture—ghastly! But it seemed right for Father. Have you noticed how Robert's getting so like Father? All that "head of the family" stuff! Father was a throw-back to the Victorian age and Robert's taking after him. I don't know how poor Ethel puts up with him.'

They reached the second floor and went into the living-room of the flat Philippa had made for herself, which overlooked the tree-lined square below. The trees were bare now and the grass soggy after a particularly wet December, but in summer the outlook was green and pleasant.

'This is much better.' Chloe sank into a chair covered in orange linen as Philippa switched on the electric fire. 'You've made it really comfy. Oh, you've got new cushion-covers. Nice. Liberty, aren't they?' As PA to a director of an important textile company with a branch in Paris, there wasn't much Chloe didn't know about materials.

'Umm—I found the stuff at a sale. Oh, Chloe, it's lovely to have you here, even if you can only stay tonight. It's so long since I've seen you.' Chloe was a tonic after the last awful weeks when Father had hovered between life and death.

'I'll try to come more often now,' Chloe promised, and Philippa knew what she meant. Chloe had got away from Father's domination and struck out for herself when she was only in her teens. She had prospered, but Father had never approved of what he had called her "way of life", and visits had become more and more infrequent, especially since Chloe had gone to work in Paris.

'Oh, I hope you will,' Philippa said and sighed for a moment's memory of how it had been when she had been a little girl and Chloe, six years older, had seemed like the mother she'd never known. 'Like a cup of tea, Sis? We'll get ourselves a meal later.'

Chloe waved a hand airily. '*Ça, c'est une très bonne idée*! My French is coming on rather well, don't you think? Of course, having a live-in lover helps. You must come over and meet Claude—he's quite something.' She kissed her fingers and flicked them towards the ceiling.

Philippa stopped on her way to the kitchen. 'Claude? What happened to François?'

Her sister made a little moue of regret. 'What always happens in the end, I fear. After a while we—ran out of steam, to put it crudely. François and I are still good friends, which is nice.'

She got up and followed Philippa into the small room that served as a kitchen, with a sink and a little electric grill and kettle.

Chloe leaned gracefully against the door-frame. 'Did you really mean it, about keeping on the printing business, Pippa? Or were you just trying to cut Robert down to size?'

Philippa filled the kettle and switched it on. 'Oh, I meant it, every word of it.' She was still a little surprised at what had happened but she was getting more used to the new, independent Philippa now. 'I'm going to enjoy having a company of my own—being the boss.' She smiled wryly and added, 'For the first time in my life.'

Chloe nodded slowly. 'Yes, I see what you mean. Working for Father must have been a fairly crushing experience.'

'Too true,' Philippa said feelingly. 'He never altogether lost that masterful captain-of-industry approach. I suppose he couldn't adjust to not being the powerful chairman of a thriving company.' She sighed.

'Poor Father—I don't think he could ever quite believe that the old family firm had failed.'

Chloe nodded. '"Old" is the right word. He never moved with the times—that's why the firm packed up. How did he get on with the men in the printing shop here? It must have been a come-down for him, only having three subordinates to manage after lording it over ten times that many.'

Philippa pulled a face. 'He didn't go down too well with the men. I found myself acting as a peacemaker quite a bit. The staff turnover was quite dramatic; only Ernie Smith, our head printer, wasn't put off by Father's winning ways. Ernie's a treasure—I couldn't get along without him.'

'And do you really think you can make a go of it on your own? Robert seemed to think the company was going downhill.'

'We're not exactly thriving just now,' Philippa admitted. Then she raised her firm little chin. She was beginning to feel a new energy and optimism blowing through her like a warm spring wind. 'But it's just a bad patch—we'll get through.'

Her sister regarded her curiously. 'You're really keen on the business, aren't you? You could sell up, as Robert suggests, and live quite well on the proceeds. Have a good time. You haven't had much fun, have you, Pippa?'

'Running my own business is going to be fun,' Philippa insisted. She struck a comic attitude. 'I'm an owner-manager now. Isn't that what they call it?'

'Ye-es…' Chloe drawled doubtfully. 'But a *printing* business! All those oily machines—and the smell of ink—and the noise!' She wrinkled her perfect small nose. 'Now if it were a boutique—or a florist's—or something like that. That would be more like you.'

Philippa chuckled. 'I work in the office, not in the printing shop. And boutiques are ten a penny—here today and gone tomorrow. I want something permanent.' The kettle boiled and she began to fill the pot.

'Then why not try marriage? I'm sure you'd have lots of eager swains if you went out and about more. I know that Derek turned out badly, but you mustn't let one mistake, years ago, put you off men for good, little sister. Isn't there anyone in the offing at present?'

Philippa's mouth quirked ruefully as she shook her head. 'It wouldn't have been easy, with Father around. He was about as welcoming as a Rottweiler if any of the customers looked my way. Not that I was partial to any of them, I hasten to add.' Her mouth softened. 'I think really Father was afraid I'd leave him on his own, and I had to make allowances. Losing the family business was a terrible blow to him. He was never the same afterwards. He sort of leaned on me, although he bossed me around.'

'I know. You have to face it, Pippa, he was a monster of selfishness. He used you.'

Philippa sighed. 'Perhaps. But no more. Philippa will be no man's slave. Which means that marriage is definitely not on the agenda. Not until I find a man who doesn't manipulate me for his own ends—and that will probably be never.'

She carried the tea-tray into the living-room and the two girls sat down on the sofa. A rather overweight black and white cat suddenly emerged from nowhere and took up a sitting position on the carpet before them, with an air of confident expectancy.

'Bully,' Philippa accused fondly, stroking his white vest. 'I know what you want.'

Chloe laughed as Philippa got up to fetch a tin of cat-snacks from the kitchen and doled them out on to a saucer, from which the cat crunched them noisily. 'Even Portly holds you in the palm of his paw—if his paw has a palm. You *are* an old softy, Pippa, love.' Impulsively she leaned over and hugged her sister and Philippa hugged her back.

They drank their tea in silence for a few minutes. Then Chloe returned to the attack. 'Well, if not marriage, what will you do?'

'Do—what should I do?' Philippa's big grey eyes widened. 'Do about what?'

'Well, you don't intend to live like a nun for the rest of your life, I take it. Look at you! You're twenty-one, aren't you? And definitely nubile.'

'Thanks,' grinned Philippa. 'Well, what do you suggest?'

Chloe sipped her tea. 'There's only one alternative to marriage, of course: affairs.'

'In the plural?' Philippa teased.

'Oh, no. Definitely one at a time. There's a lot to be said for affairs. They're heavenly at the beginning.' She wriggled sensuously. 'And you go on together just as long as you want to and then, some time, you both begin to fall for someone else. And you part friends.'

'And it starts all over again?'

'Um, that's the idea,' Chloe said complacently.

'I'm not sure,' Philippa said, 'that affairs are quite *me*, if you know what I mean.' To put it any stronger than that and to say that the thought of a series of affairs repelled her would seem like criticising her sister's way of life, and she would hate to do that. 'Another cup of tea?'

Chloe passed her cup over. 'You wait,' she said darkly. 'One day you'll see a stranger across a crowded room and all that jazz.'

'I hope not, it would complicate things far too much just now. I want to belong to myself. No man on the scene to take charge of me.' She stretched her arms wide and her grey eyes glistened. 'Oh, Chloe, it's wonderful to feel free. I've no intention of taking dear Robert's advice, though I suppose he meant well and wanted to help.'

Chloe looked sceptical. 'I doubt it. He's growing into an authority figure, like Father.' She shook her head slowly, her eyes resting on her young sister's slender form in its clinging grey dress. 'The trouble is, you're such a little thing; you've got that kind of vulnerable look that makes men want to look after you.'

Or bully me, Philippa thought. 'You mean I'm a wimp?' she demanded, suddenly acting fierce. 'You just wait. I'm going to be a successful businesswoman from now on, running my own life, taking no orders from anyone—especially if that anyone is male.'

'Well said!' Chloe laughed. 'Let me know how you get on. And if you need a bit of relaxation from the daily grind come over to Paris and I'll introduce you to a nice sexy Frenchman.'

Philippa's eyes sparkled with mischief. 'I might take you up on that. You really think an affair is what I need?'

'*Mais certainement*,' said Chloe with her best French accent. 'Think about it.'

* * *

It was a long, long time since Philippa had allowed herself to remember Derek, and what had happened three years ago, but talking to Chloe had brought it all back and that night, as she lay in bed, she found herself remembering what at the time had been a ghastly nightmare.

She had fallen romantically in love with Derek just before her nineteenth birthday. Father had still owned the wholesale hardware company then, and Derek had been starting out in his own insurance business. They had met at the large Solihull house which had been home then, one summer evening when Derek had called to see Father. Philippa had been dazzled by Derek's dark good looks and dashing manner. After the interview was over Derek had asked to see the garden, and they had walked together in the dusk, with the scent of roses all around. He had slipped his arm round her shoulders and his brown eyes had smouldered into hers and awakened new and over-whelming emotions.

She'd left school a month previously and was waiting to start at university in September, but she had never started at university. She had got engaged to Derek in a haze of bliss, blinded by the sure belief that he loved her as she loved him. They had arranged to be married on her nineteenth birthday.

In her new happiness she had even found the strength to hold out against Father's disapproval. He hadn't liked Derek, and, looking back now, she felt that if his business hadn't been on the verge of collapse he would have put his foot down more heavily. But perhaps he'd been relieved to think that she would have a husband to take her off his hands when the crash came.

Lying in the dark now, she wondered why she had to think about Derek and that awful time. Perhaps because she was determined to make a new start, finally to wipe that episode from her memory, like wiping a tape clean by recording a new message over what had been on it before.

She would allow herself just once more to recall Derek's expression when he had walked out on her, his handsome face drawn into mean, vicious lines. 'A good thing I found out before we got married. Your father's broke—didn't he have the guts to tell you? He'd have let us go on and get married if I hadn't got wind of the state of his affairs and tackled him. I suppose the bastard wanted to include his daughter with the bankrupt stock,' he'd sneered.

He'd told her the truth brutally. He'd expected to be made a partner in Father's business, and to take it over when Father retired. That had been his sole reason for marrying her. 'When I think I might have been landed with a soppy little virgin and nothing to gain from it! Well, don't expect to see me waiting at the altar.'

He'd been drinking heavily and he had spat the words out crudely before he slammed out of the house, leaving Philippa shivering with sick, shocked misery.

It was all over long ago and she didn't feel bitter about it. She felt as if it had happened to somebody else, a very naïve young girl who had allowed herself to be tricked by her emotions. Never again, she vowed, would she allow a man to use her for his own selfish ends. In future dealings with any man she would be very, very careful.

*   *   *

The house seemed quiet after Chloe had left for the airport next morning. Philippa decided to start straight away on a thorough examination of the firm's financial position. By the end of the afternoon the books were up to date. Things were rather worse than she'd expected, but all firms had their ups and downs, she told herself. She'd have to think up some way of attracting more business. A large advert in the local free paper might be a start.

The phone rang and her spirits rose. An order? 'The Albany Press,' she said brightly. 'What can I do for you?'

'How are you, Pippa?' said Robert. 'And how are things? I thought I'd give you a ring.'

'Oh, I'm fine—fine,' Philippa said, pushing down her disappointment. 'I hope Ethel's well.'

'She's got one of her migraines,' Robert said, adding irritably, 'they're getting a damn nuisance.'

Philippa murmured something sympathetic, but Robert wasn't listening. 'What I want to tell you, Pippa, is that I've arranged with a colleague of mine to call on you. His name is Bartholomew Marchant and he's head of an important firm of management consultants. He'll look into things for you and give you his opinion of the business—you really must have expert advice if you're determined to try to carry on on your own. Marchant lives in your direction, and he's promised to look in on you on his way home this evening. You can have a preliminary chat and arrange a time for him to go into all the details.'

Philippa felt anger boiling up inside her. 'But Robert, I don't *want* to see this man,' she began. 'I don't *need* any help. I told you——'

'Sorry, must go. I've got someone waiting to see me. Let me know how you get on. Goodbye, Pippa.' Robert had rung off.

Philippa glared at the telephone receiver in frustration and slammed the old-fashioned black instrument back on its cradle.

She'd thought—hoped—that Robert would leave her alone, at least for a short time. But no! A short twenty-four hours had passed and already he was interfering, sending this...this trouble-shooter person to pry into the books and find out how things were—and no doubt report back to Robert.

What was she going to do? She would *not* see the Marchant individual. She absolutely refused to have some man poking his nose into the books, snooping round the printing shop down in the basement—putting the mens' backs up. No, she would jolly well send him away before he even set foot over the doorstep, however angry that would make Robert.

She sat in Father's huge director-type chair, her slender body very straight in its white blouse and grey skirt, and glared belligerently out of the window at the tight row of diagonally parked cars in the service road, standing with their noses towards the squelchy grass in the square. Mr Snoopy Marchant wouldn't find anywhere to park when he arrived, she thought with grim satisfaction.

How *dared* Robert interfere, after what she'd said to him? After she'd made it crystal-clear...? Philippa shook her head in helpless fury, and the bow that she wore in the office came untied, releasing a fall of silky dark hair on to her shoulders. Impatiently she tied it up again. When this person arrived she had to look like a confident young owner-manager, which was her

new image, not like the teenager she sometimes
thought she saw when she looked in the mirror. She
considered it a great drawback to look younger than
she was.

Now Father was no longer here it was becoming
clear that Robert was expecting to take over her life
and arrange it for her. Oh, no, she vowed, she was
certainly not going to be 'guided' by Robert. And for
'guided' read 'pushed around', she thought wrath-
fully. Probably all very large men had a power
complex where small women were concerned.

I won't have it, I *won't*. Philippa beat her small
fists on the huge mahogany desk, and even the solid
glass paperweights rattled.

The nerve of him! You can have a preliminary chat!
'Oh, no, I can't have a preliminary chat,' Philippa
muttered between clenched teeth. 'Not on your life!
I intend to show Mr Bartholomew Marchant exactly
where he gets off.'

She'd be polite, of course, regretful. Her brother
had made a mistake. I don't really need any help.
Thank you for calling, Mr Marchant, I do hope it
hasn't taken you out of your way...

Rehearsing his dismissal, Philippa went into the hall
and closed the front door. It was left open in the
daytime, with a notice on the inner porch door, 'Please
enter', and another notice inside saying 'Office'. Not
having a secretary or a receptionist, that was the only
way Philippa could deal with customers now she was
working alone. But at least she could make sure that
this Marchant person would not get into the house.

The front door firmly closed, she climbed upstairs
to her flat to make sure her image was as near as she
could make it to that of the cool, confident young

executive who was very shortly going to send Robert's Nosy Parker 'colleague' about his business.

Half an hour later Bartholomew Marchant—Bart to his friends—parked his wicked-looking black Jaguar in a space just vacated, swung his long legs out of the driving seat, locked the door and stood looking up at number sixteen, Albany Square, all five storeys of it. The first thing his raking blue glance took in was that the façade was badly in need of repair. The fronts of the adjoining houses had recently been renovated, but the front of number sixteen showed ominous cracks, the attractive wrought-iron railings of the first-floor balcony were badly in need of paint, the stucco round the windows was crumbling and in places missing altogether, disclosing the brickwork beneath. He didn't wonder that Robert Price was sceptical of continuing to keep a viable business operating from a run-down address like this.

Bart was fond of Leamington, which town claimed, among other contenders, to be the Heart of England. It was proud of its heritage, its gracefully curving parade, its pump-rooms, its squares and crescents.

Times had changed, of course, as he admitted with a faintly regretful sigh. Once, carriages would have drawn up outside the imposing porticoed entrances in the square, and footmen would have escorted elegant ladies to be driven to the classically decorated pump-room restaurant. There, to the accompaniment of soft music from a three-piece band behind the potted palms, they would take tea and exchange gossip with their friends.

He grinned to himself at his fancy. This was the end of the twentieth century. The tall houses in Albany

Square had been duly 'developed' into luxury flats—
their vertical rows of small name-plates were evidence
of it. Number sixteen was the exception, he noted.
Here a single brass plate on the iron railings announced 'The Albany Press'. He looked down over
the railings to the semi-basement. All was in darkness
inside, but he thought he could make out the shadowy
shape of printing presses, and he reacted as he always
did to anything connected with printing. With lively
curiosity. He would certainly enjoy helping Robert
Price's sister, and the printing connection was an
added interest.

Then he looked a little closer. Good lord, the
shadowy shapes below had become clearer and had
formed themselves into a recognisable printing press.
He was fairly sure it was a hand-set letter-press ma-
chine, the kind that had been out of fashion for commercial use for donkey's years. If he was right it was
no wonder that Robert Price was worried about the
viability of the company.

Bart ran lightly up the three front steps to the important front door, grasped the bell-pull on its long
chain, and heard its summons jangling somewhere
inside the house. While he waited he recalled what
Robert Price had said about his sister. 'Poor child,
she's had a bad time, trying to cope with everything
since our father was taken ill. She's been working in
the office with Father since she left secretarial college.
She's a brave little thing, but I'm afraid it's all been
too much for her.' He'd shaken his head sadly. 'And
now she's got this crack-brained idea that she can
manage a run-down business all by herself. Try to talk
her out of it, Bart, for everybody's sake.'

As he heard light footsteps approaching along the hall Bart Marchant arranged his lean, intelligent face into a pleasant smile.

He didn't expect the job to be too difficult. And the outcome might—just might—be in his own favour. An intriguing idea was beginning to take shape in his mind. If he played his cards right he might come out of this commission with something definitely to his own advantage.

CHAPTER TWO

PHILIPPA ran lightly down the stairs to the hall. The adrenalin was still putting a delicate pink in her cheeks. She'd soon see off this intruder. She visualised him as short and weedy, with mousy hair, a sharp nose and gold-rimmed spectacles. If she stood on the top step she would be able to look him straight in the eye and... She pulled open the heavy door.

Oh, lord, was her first horrified thought, she couldn't have been more wrong.

He was wearing a dark business suit and his legs seemed to go down a long, long way. Short he was *not*. Even though he was standing on the step below her, Philippa had to look up to his face; he must be well over six feet tall. She'd been wrong about everything else too. His hair was brown but certainly not mousy, rather the colour of teak, not too short and not too long, and its tendency to curl was evidently kept in check by firm brushing. His nose was on the large and dominant side, and his heavily lashed blue eyes obviously didn't need the assistance of spectacles, gold-rimmed or otherwise.

And, although it had nothing to do with the matter in hand, somewhere inside Philippa's head was registered the fact that he was probably the most attractive man she'd seen for a long, long time.

She thrust the thought aside. Her first job was to adjust to the new situation, which was even worse than she had expected. She hadn't wanted a management consultant of any kind, and she certainly wasn't going to have any dealings with a management consultant who towered above her even higher than Father or Robert.

'Miss Price?' His voice was very deep, friendly, reassuring. He held out his hand. 'Bartholomew Marchant.'

She didn't recall inviting him into the house, but somehow they were standing in the hall together. 'Your brother phoned to say I was coming?'

She found that her hand was engulfed in his large hand. His touch was cool and dynamic. The physical effect of it wriggled up her arm and down to her toes. The man was overwhelming; he must be got rid of as quickly as possible.

She swallowed hard. 'Mr Marchant, I...'

'That's right,' he said. 'Only please make it Bart, as I'm a family friend—sort of. Your brother and I are mortal enemies on the squash court. This is your office, is it?'

By now he had got himself into the office, and was standing beside the desk. Dazedly Philippa thought that he seemed to fill the large, high room with his dominating masculine presence. Even more than Father had done. This wouldn't do at all. 'I think I should tell you before we go any further...' she began again.

Then he smiled at her and her voice seemed to trickle away. He had beautiful teeth and his mouth curved at one side when he smiled. 'Suppose we take it slowly?' he said. 'Let's just sit down and get to know each other, hm?'

He was standing behind Father's imposing director's chair, his hands on the back of it. Just as if he had taken charge of the place! He was *not* going to sit in Father's chair—that would be the final straw.

Philippa moved hastily around the desk to sit in the big chair herself. To her annoyance, he pulled it out for her to seat herself, and then walked round to sit in the visitor's chair beside the desk. Just as if he had meant to do that all along! He was devious, she told herself. He was laying on the charm to get her confidence, then he would start in on the demolition work. She was certain that that was why Robert had sent him. All that talk about helping her with running the business had been eyewash.

He glanced round the big room, keen blue eyes taking in the elaborate cornice, the huge open fireplace and its carved wooden mantel and tiled surround, the ancient green metal filing cabinets, the vast mahogany desk, carefully arranged by Philippa to hide the most worn part of the carpet.

'Fascinating—these old houses,' he said chattily. 'Early nineteenth century, I should think—the age of gracious living.'

'Oh, yes?' Philippa said coldly. She didn't know much about gracious living. Living and working for Father had been a chilly, almost formal experience.

'And your printing shop is in the basement? A convenient arrangement—to have your office just above.'

Philippa said nothing.

'Your brother was saying you've lived here alone since your father died.'

'Yes,' said Philippa, lifting her chin a fraction. 'I intend to take a couple of girl students in the upstairs rooms later on.' She wasn't going to tell him that that idea had just come to her this moment. Her tone suggested that it had nothing to do with him.

Bartholomew Marchant smiled at her again, and as she saw the way his blue eyes squeezed up she felt a curious limpness around her knees, which were mercifully tucked out of sight beneath the desk. He said, 'You're resenting me, aren't you? Why? Is it a case of hate at first sight?'

He'd given her the opening she needed. 'Of course not,' she said, taking a deep breath. 'It's my brother Robert I'm resenting, if resentment's the right word. He had no right to ask you to come here to—to "look into things" was the way he put it. I told him I wanted to be left alone to run the business in my own way but he insists on treating me like a child. I'm sorry, Mr Marchant, but I'm afraid it's put you in a false position. I don't need help—and I certainly don't want anybody looking into things for me.'

He was sitting back in his chair while she delivered this speech. In the dusk of the winter afternoon his eyes were fixed on her with an expression that unnerved her slightly. She sensed that he was—what? Angry? Disappointed? Puzzled? But whatever he was feeling he had himself tightly under control.

She got to her feet. 'So...' She allowed the hint to hover in the air between them.

He uncoiled his long body from the chair and Philippa wished she hadn't been so eager to stand up herself. She seemed to sense a threat in him as he towered above her. Ridiculous, of course; he'd go in a moment and then she wouldn't see him again. All the same...

'I see,' he said formally. 'I wouldn't want to interfere in any way in the business affairs here without your prior consent. There has evidently been some misunderstanding.'

There was a long silence and Philippa could think of nothing to say. Why didn't he just *go*, instead of standing there looking down at her as if she were some sort of weirdo? She began to wonder if her eye-shadow had smudged or if the bow with which she had hastily tied back her dark hair, in an effort to present the image of a self-sufficient young career woman, had slipped again. She had to restrain herself from putting up a hand to find out.

At last he spoke, and it was in a completely different voice, relaxed, with a lurking touch of humour. 'I'm afraid we've got off to a bad start, haven't we? I suggest we get to know each other a little better before we tackle any business problems, and what better way than to exchange views over a meal? So... will you give me the pleasure of buying dinner for you, Pippa?'

Her head jerked back and her eyes flew open.

'The name's Philippa,' she said in as chilly a voice as she could manage.

'Sorry—Philippa,' he amended. 'Your brother spoke of you as Pippa. Well, Philippa—how about it?'

'I have work to do.' She gestured towards the desk, which was all too tidy and didn't suggest a heavy workload waiting for her.

'Nothing you couldn't do tomorrow, I'm sure,' he said smoothly. 'Do take pity on me. It's my housekeeper's day off and I intended to eat in Leamington— at the Regent Hotel, if that's agreeable to you.'

Philippa began to feel that she was being subtly attacked. Was this the way management consultants worked—putting things on a friendly, relaxed footing, before they told you that your business was on the rocks? And if they were dealing with a woman they *would* put on the charm—just as this man was doing. Effortlessly. Dangerously. He'd already shown that he could manipulate her. Look at the way he'd got himself into the house without being asked! This dinner invitation was surely an underhand way to play Robert's game. She didn't like the man and she certainly didn't trust him.

'Do come,' he said, and smiled at her. A confident smile that made her simmer with anger. He wouldn't expect to be refused by a woman. Well, he was going to be refused by her. 'Thank you very much, Mr Marchant,' she said in a clear, high voice. 'But I prefer not to come out this evening.'

That was straight from the shoulder. She saw the way the smile disappeared from his face, leaving a look of—what was it? Surely not hurt? For a split-second she felt a twinge of guilt and then pushed it away. This man had come here to pry, she reminded herself, so he shouldn't be surprised to get a firm brush-off.

'I'm sorry,' he said, and added the conventional, 'Perhaps some other time?'

Equally conventional, she added coolly, 'Perhaps.' She walked with him into the hall and opened the front door. He descended two steps and turned. A polite goodbye hovered on Philippa's lips. Their faces were on a level now as their eyes met. Then he gestured towards the basement. 'Would it be possible to take a quick look round your printing shop while I'm here? I'm interested in printing.'

Philippa gasped. The cheek of the man! She said dismissively, 'There's nobody there—the men have gone home.'

'Oh. Oh, yes, of course.' He looked so disappointed that she could almost believe it was genuine. Surely he wouldn't think she would be taken in by so obvious a ruse to worm his way into the firm's affairs?

He descended the last step to the pavement. 'Oh, dear,' he said ruefully, and now he *was* looking up at her. 'That was a foolish thing to suggest. I'll look forward to seeing it when your staff are here.'

Philippa breathed hard to control the biting rejoinder that almost burst out. The man must have the hide of a rhinoceros to invite himself to return.

He waited a moment, but when she didn't reply he said amiably, 'Well, I'll be getting along, then.' He moved towards the black Jaguar parked a few yards down the service road. 'Goodnight, Philippa. Don't work too hard,' he called cheerfully over his shoulder.

'Goodbye,' she replied frostily.

She went in and closed the door, conscious that her breathing was fast and uneven. That was a narrow escape, she told herself. She had almost allowed the old weakness to overtake her, to let herself be manipulated by a strong masculine magnetism again.

She heard the whirr of a self-starter, the growl of a powerful car engine. As the sound faded away she walked slowly back into the office. Suddenly she felt desperately tired. She'd have a bath and a light supper and go to bed early.

Tomorrow she must face the challenge of trying to keep her printing business from closing down. *Without* the help of Mr Snoopy Bartholomew Marchant, she added to herself, trying to summon a smile.

But somehow that gibe didn't seem in the least funny any more.

* * *

Driving away, Bart Marchant narrowed his deep-set blue eyes as he watched the road, but his thoughts were on the girl he had just left. He'd got quite a wrong impression from Robert Price of his young sister. He'd built up a picture of a fragile, pliant young girl with a foolish idea that she was capable of running a company on her own. He hadn't expected too much resistance to his usual professional approach. He had found that most women reacted favourably to what he thought of, with wry self-mockery, as the 'bedside manner' that came easily to him. Not that beds featured in it literally, of course; he was careful about that.

But little Miss Price had been no easy option. He had an uncomfortable feeling that those incredible grey eyes had looked him over, summed him up, and had certainly not been impressed by what they had seen. And underneath the very feminine, not to say alluring, exterior he had sensed a hint of steel. Interesting! She presented a challenge, and he enjoyed challenges. He hadn't got very far on this first occasion but there would be other occasions very soon. He was a little surprised how much that certainty intrigued him.

The following day Ernie Smith, head printer, arrived early as usual, partly so that he would be able to find a parking-space, but mostly because he loved his job. Philippa was in the office even earlier and was waiting by the window when he parked his lovingly polished ancient MG in the service road. She knocked on the window, beckoning to him to come straight to the office instead of going down the basement steps to the printing shop.

He joined her in the office. Ernie Smith was a smallish middle-aged man with bristly, reddish hair and a gruff manner which concealed, as Philippa well knew, a heart of gold.

'Good morning, Ernie,' she said. 'Come in.' She waved towards a chair. 'We have to talk.'

His slightly protuberant brown eyes surveyed the litter on her desk as he sat down beside it. 'Bills?' he queried knowingly.

'Too true, and too many.' Philippa shuffled the pile together. 'Ernie, we seem to have what is known as a cash-flow problem. And orders are drying up a bit, aren't they? Why do you think that is?'

'Competition,' Ernie said ruefully. 'Twice as many printing firms round here as there were five years ago.'

'But we're supposed to be a boom town—with the new motorway and the technical park and everything. There should be lots more business around; why can't we attract it? You and the other two do a marvellous job. I don't understand.'

Ernie rubbed his nose and looked down at the carpet.

'Don't pull any punches, Ernie.' Philippa planted her elbows on the desk and leaned towards him. 'I have to know the whole story.'

He seemed to make up his mind. 'We're out of date, luv; we need capital investment for new presses. Should have had it long ago.' He coughed apologetically. 'I told your father, you know. But he saw it different, like, and I couldn't shift him.'

Philippa sighed. 'No, I don't suppose you could.' When Father dug his heels in over anything they stayed dug. 'I expect it was all pretty old-fashioned even when he bought it.'

Ernie nodded dolefully. 'It's the time it takes to get the stuff out, you see. We're in the electronic age and what we're doing here is the way they did it a hundred years ago. It's not that the presses wear out—they'd probably last forever—it's just that the technical side of things has changed so much. And we can't do colour work—which everyone wants these days.'

Philippa groaned. 'Well, tell me the worst, Ernie. What do you need and how much will it cost?'

He brightened. 'You mean it's on the cards that we can go ahead?'

'I don't know yet. I'll have to beard the bank manager in his den.' She tried to sound jokey but inside she was quaking. Mr Williams hadn't been as amiable as usual last time she had gone to talk to him about extending the overdraft. 'Can you let me have a run-down on prices later this morning and I'll make an appointment to see him this afternoon if I can?'

Ernie jumped up. 'Will do. I'll ring round the suppliers straight away and get one or two different options mapped out, OK?'

'OK.' Philippa nodded. 'And Ernie——' as he hurried towards the door.

He turned, beaming at her. He was so good, so loyal, and he looked like an eager little terrier dog. She couldn't bring herself to say what she ought to say: Don't bank on it too much. 'It doesn't matter, it'll do later,' she substituted.

He nodded, and a moment or two later she heard him running down the steps to the basement.

Philippa rested her elbows on the big desk and stared out of the window. The situation was worse than she'd expected and it looked as if only the bank could save them now. What, she wondered, would

Bartholomew Marchant have advised—if she'd agreed to let him advise her? He was the kind of man who wouldn't stand any nonsense from bank managers, she was sure of that.

Rather to her annoyance she had found herself thinking about him far too often since their interview. He was a man you didn't forget in a hurry. She closed her eyes now and she could see him again, sitting in the chair across the desk, as he had sat yesterday—relaxed and powerful, with magnetic dark blue eyes in a lean, intelligent face, a quizzical smile and beautiful manners.

And sexy—oh, yes, she recognised that. She closed her eyes and a small shiver ran down her spine as she remembered that long, mobile mouth and how it had curved up at one corner when he smiled.

She opened her eyes and shook herself. What was she doing, wasting time thinking about a man she would probably never see again?

She glanced at the clock over the mantelpiece—it was too early yet to ring the bank. She picked up a Biro and began to scribble down figures, to see where she could do a little manipulation before she faced Mr Williams, the bank manager.

At half-past five that same afternoon it was pouring with rain as Philippa returned from a frustrating interview with the bank manager. She'd been so angry when she came out of the bank that she couldn't trust herself to go home straight away and tell Ernie what Mr Williams had said. A cup of strong tea at Rackham's in the parade had calmed her down slightly, but she was still tensed up when she got back to Albany Square.

She ran headlong down the outside entrance to the basement, the heels of her black boots clicking on the stone steps, the scarlet of her woollen jacket flashing like a danger signal against the stained off-white of the stucco wall.

In front of the basement door she stopped to pull herself together, breathing hard. Bank managers! she thought in disgust. They were supposed to encourage small businesses to invest, weren't they? But all *he'd* done was talk about how prosperous the business had been when her father was running it, and what a pity that they were now finding it difficult to get orders. He hadn't seemed to listen when she'd explained that orders had been falling off for the past year or so, even when Father had been in charge.

He'd pretended to be sympathetic but beneath all the smooth talk she'd heard the unspoken comment that a young girl was hardly equipped to run a printing business on her own. She'd wanted to yell at him that she wasn't a young girl, she was a woman of nearly twenty-two, but she hadn't supposed that would help matters. So she'd fallen back on the argument that with modern equipment they could increase their business substantially, but he hadn't seemed impressed by it. The trouble was, she wasn't altogether impressed by it herself. And Ernie's estimates of the cost of new presses had been far higher than she'd expected.

Finally Mr Williams had pursed his lips and informed her, with a great show of reluctance, that the bank really couldn't see its way to offer a loan for the purpose of investment. And had ended up with a veiled threat that if things didn't improve the bank might have to consider calling in the overdraft.

'Beast!' Philippa muttered now as she turned the handle of the basement door.

The printing shop had long ago been the kitchen quarters of the old house. It consisted of three rooms. The largest housed the main presses, the next one was used for storage and some of the old presses no longer in use, and the third was a general-purpose room where the men could hang their coats, make tea and eat lunch if they didn't want to go out for it. The atmosphere of the printing shop met Philippa as she went in: the warm smell of damp and printers' ink; the heavy presses that certainly seemed more in keeping with the industrial revolution than the end of the twentieth century; the massive composing table; the wooden cupboards and drawers; the stacks of paper. It was all so familiar. And it was hers now. She couldn't bear to think of it closing down.

A single strip-light lit up one end of the room. Ernie was bending over the larger of the two presses, a cleaning rag in his hand. Ted and Wayne must have gone home early. There was a horrid hint of a firm in decline about the place.

He looked up quickly when she went in. She saw the question in his face and shook her head dolefully. 'No go, I'm afraid, Ernie. He wouldn't agree to a loan. We'll have to struggle on with the presses we've got.'

Ernie coughed gently; he seemed slightly embarrassed.

And then, from the shadows of the adjoining room, looking very much at home, stepped Bartholomew Marchant.

Philippa was conscious of a jolt under her diaphragm.

'Hello, Philippa, I took you up on your permission to have a look around your printing shop.'

'Oh,' said Philippa, and added stupidly, 'Did you?' She didn't recall giving him any permission.

He smiled at her and under the strip-light his teeth looked very white against his suntanned cheeks. Suntan—in January? Of course—he'd have all the money in the world to spend on skiing holidays, or lying on some tropical beach, she told herself sourly, not wanting to admit that his smile was doing uncomfortable things to her inside. 'I've been having a wonderful time,' he enthused. 'Ernie has been kindly showing me everything.'

Ernie grinned widely. 'Mr Marchant is really interested in all the old machines. Very knowledgeable you are too, sir, if you don't mind me saying so.'

'I take it as a compliment—coming from an expert,' Bartholomew Marchant beamed.

Great! Very cosy! Philippa fumed inwardly. The wretched man's got Ernie on his side without any effort.

'You're keen on museum pieces, Mr Marchant?' She arched a perfect brow in his direction.

'If that's what these are, then the answer is yes,' he said. 'And there's something even closer to my heart.' He walked towards the shadowy side of the room. 'I see you've even got an original Albion.' He put a hand on the heavy iron handpress, with the same kind of awed reverence with which a vintage-car addict might lay a finger on the bonnet of a 1920 Rolls-Royce.

Ernie joined him. 'Ah, we pensioned off that old lady a good while ago, sir. Not but what she couldn't still do her stuff OK, but she's not quite up to life in the fast lane.' He chuckled at his own joke.

'I suppose not,' Bart admitted. 'It's all high-tech now, of course.'

For a minute or two words like computer type-setting and photolitho and desk-top publishing rolled off Ernie's tongue lovingly. Philippa herself knew very little about the actual processes of printing, but she began to realise how much Ernie had been held back by having to work with out-of-date equipment. Perhaps, she thought dismally, she ought to take Robert's advice and wind up the company. Would Ernie and the other two manage to find new jobs if she did?

She turned to the door, biting her lip when she felt the foolish tears prick behind her eyelids. It had been a beastly day.

'I'll see you in the morning, Ernie,' she said in a small voice. 'Goodnight.' She included Bartholomew Marchant vaguely.

But he was at the door first, opening it for her. 'Cheerio, Ernie; I'll look in again if you'll let me.'

'Delighted, sir,' beamed the renegade Ernie. Philippa couldn't blame him—he didn't know the background of Mr Snoopy Marchant.

Philippa had chosen to leave by the outside door, rather than the one that led up directly to the office through the house. If the Marchant man followed her out then she could take leave of him on the pavement, rather than let him insinuate himself into the house again as he'd done yesterday. It was, she knew, stupid to allow his presence to disturb her as it was doing. It wasn't as if she liked the man; in fact she disliked him actively, and even more so because he must have known that she had never intended to issue any sort of invitation to him to look over the printing shop.

She marched up the basement steps and was aware that he was following her. At the top she half turned with a dismissive smile. 'Well, good evening, Mr...'

He put his hand on her arm and she was conscious of a slight shiver running through her. It was fear; it must be. It couldn't be anything...different, could it?

'Look, Philippa,' he said forcefully. 'Let's cut out the small talk, shall we? I have something which I think rather important to say to you. May I come in?'

Taken aback by his change of tone, Philippa almost said, No, you can't, and slammed the door in his face. She remembered all the hectoring she'd suffered from Father. She wasn't going to take even the least hint of it from this man.

But she had to make it absolutely clear to him that his presence wasn't welcome here, and she couldn't do that standing on the pavement.

She shrugged. 'All right, come in,' she said not very graciously, and led the way up to the front door with an impatient swish of her grey pleated skirt round her slim, elegant legs. Perhaps it was as well that she didn't witness the interested gleam in Bart Marchant's blue eyes as he followed her up the steps.

CHAPTER THREE

IN THE office, Philippa waved towards the chair Bart had occupied yesterday. Inbuilt good manners made her ask, 'Would you like a drink?' She pulled off her scarlet jacket, shook the rain from it, and hung it on one of the curly arms of the mahogany coat-stand behind the door.

'Thank you, a small whisky, if that's OK.'

Father had always kept whisky in the cupboard beside the filing cabinet. She poured a measure into a glass and took it over to the man seated at the desk. 'Water?'

'Thanks, just a drop.'

'I'll get some from the kitchen,' Philippa said, and turned to the door.

'No, please don't bother, I'll have it neat.' He put a restraining hand on her arm and she stopped dead. Here it was again—the feeling that a powerful charge of electricity was running right up her arm.

Oh, no, she thought desperately. I can't cope with this. She sank into Father's big chair, drawing in a deep breath.

Bart took a pull at his whisky and put his glass down. 'Aren't you joining me?'

Philippa's throat felt dry. 'I...' The sound came out high and squeaky and she started again. 'I had some tea in town.'

40

Perceptive dark blue eyes studied her face. 'After your interview with the bank manager? Was it all that bad?' he said softly.

She met his gaze with dislike. 'Extra-sensory perception? Or just plain guesswork?'

'Neither,' he said smoothly. 'Merely an ordinary faculty for putting two and two together.'

'And making fifteen,' Philippa sneered.

He refused to be goaded. 'Plus the fact that I couldn't help hearing what you said to Ernie when you came in just now.'

'Yes—well, you weren't meant to. It was—confidential. I'd no idea you were there.'

'No, I know,' he said quietly. 'If your attitude towards me so far is anything to go by, I'd hardly expect you to be taking me into your confidence.'

Philippa gave up trying to make him react; he seemed to be armour-plated against snubs. That must be his style; he probably spent his time dealing with company directors who were tearing out their hair with worry, while he remained maddeningly laid-back. The worst of it was that he made her feel petty and mean.

Philippa rather prided herself on being fair-minded. She supposed it wasn't his fault that Robert had asked him to interfere. 'I'm sorry,' she said stiffly. 'I've been rather rude. What was the important thing you wanted to say?'

A flicker of a smile touched his long, mobile lips. 'You won't like it,' he warned.

'Possibly not,' she said. 'I can guess what you're going to say. After hearing my moan about the bank manager, your expertise must have told you that the company is in difficulties. But nothing that I can't put right, I'm confident.' She hoped she sounded more confident than she felt.

'That,' he said, 'is what I propose to make up my own mind about—when you decide to let me take a look at the books.'

She was gently boiling inside at the tenacity of the man, but she wasn't going to fight with him if she could help it. She said, 'My brother Robert asked you to persuade me that I should give up the printing business, didn't he?'

'I suppose you could put it like that,' he admitted.

Suddenly she wanted to clear the air between them. 'Mr Marchant...'

'Please—Bart,' he said.

'All right, then—Bart.' It was ridiculous how saying his name gave her a breathless feeling. She cleared her throat and ploughed on, 'It may seem stupid to you, but it's very important to me that I don't let Robert interfere in my affairs. Which means—and apparently I must repeat it—that I have no intention of allowing you to examine the books of the firm. Or of accepting your professional help. I'm sorry if that sounds rude, but that's the way it's going to be.'

He'd been watching her closely as she had delivered her speech. 'I'm sorry too,' he said, so quietly that it sounded almost menacing, 'but I'm afraid I'm going to insist on seeing the books.'

'*Insist*?' The single word was enough to ignite the anger that had been smouldering. She'd managed to keep her temper so far, but no way was this man going to ride roughshod over her. 'Insist?' Her voice went up a couple of tones. 'How dare you try to bully me? You've absolutely no right to bulldoze your way in here and—and...' she was gabbling now in her fury

'...and sweet-talk my head printer to get information out of him—and throw your weight about—and—and eavesdrop on a private conversation—and then talk about *insisting*. I won't stand for it.'

She jumped to her feet, trembling, and glared down into the maddeningly impassive face that was raised to hers, dark brows lifted slightly. She was dimly aware that she should be keeping very calm herself—not screeching at him like a peevish parrot. That was the thing men criticised about women in business, wasn't it? Too emotional. No balance.

He stood up too. He would, of course—he wasn't going to allow her any advantage. 'I'm very sorry you feel like that,' he said. 'But if you think it over reasonably you'll admit that I have my job to do. Do you really want me to go back to your brother and tell him that you've been uncooperative to the point of intransigence? That won't get any of us anywhere.'

He loomed over her. He was so *big*. He made her feel weak and helpless, the way Father had sometimes used to make her feel. She felt a sudden sick stab of the old fear and put her hand to her throat. She must keep a grip on herself—she mustn't let this man bully her. This was the first test of her new independence and she mustn't fail.

She stood very straight and dignified, her chin raised a fraction. 'You can tell Robert what you like, Mr Marchant. I shall run my own business in my own way. And now, will you please leave?'

He made no move to leave. He just stood there, staring at her glassily. 'Your—did you say your own business?'

'Of course it's my own business,' she told him impatiently. 'My father left it to me. And I intend to run it myself, without any interference from my brother—or anybody else,' she added, her voice suddenly fierce.

Bart's long mouth relaxed slowly into his lop-sided grin. 'Your own business! Well, I'll be blowed! That certainly makes a difference.' He sat down again rather quickly. 'You really own the whole show?'

'I've just told you so,' Philippa said crossly. 'Would you like to see a copy of my father's will?'

He was shaking his head—in amazement, rather than as a reply to her question.

'Didn't you know?' she asked. 'Didn't Robert explain the position?'

Bart said grimly, 'Your brother will have plenty of explaining to do when I see him next. And I'll have several uncomplimentary things to say to him for putting me in a position like this. Sit down, Philippa; I can't apologise to you properly when you're standing above me like an avenging angel.'

Her spurt of temper had left her knees feeling weak, and she sank gratefully into her chair.

'As you've probably gathered,' he said, 'your brother certainly led me to believe that you were merely acting as a temporary manager here until things were straightened out.'

'Hm. And I suppose he told you I'd got this mad idea that I could manage the business on my own and I had to be talked out of it?'

He pulled a wry face. ' "Crack-brained" was the word, I'm afraid.'

'Yes, that sounds like Robert.' She warmed to the topic. 'The poor, delicate, feeble little girl who has to be saved from her own stupidity? That was what you thought you had to deal with when you arrived yesterday?'

She saw a smile hovering. 'If I did, you very quickly disabused me of that idea. A fierce little she-dragon, breathing fire and brimstone would be more like it.'

Suddenly he was serious again. 'Oh, Philippa, what can I say? Do you want me to grovel? I really am very sorry this has happened and I shudder to imagine what you must have thought of me—barging into your printing shop—trying to quiz you, insisting on examining the books.'

'I thought you were being very high-handed, but I see now that it wasn't your fault.' It surprised her how eagerly she rushed to excuse him.

It also surprised her how intensely aware of him she was—sitting just around the desk from her. If she'd put out a hand she could have touched the arm he was resting on the desk, could have felt the hard muscle beneath the fine cloth of his jacket. She felt a slow flush rise to her cheeks and looked away quickly.

He said ruefully, 'It's generous of you to take it so well. I should have liked very much for us to be friends, to work together, if necessary, in the interests of your firm. But I see now that probably isn't on the cards?' He waited, and she felt the keen blue eyes searching her face. 'Is it?'

'No,' she said firmly. 'It isn't. As you've gathered, we're going through a bad patch, but things will improve. Managing a company is something I have to learn, and I intend to learn very quickly indeed. My father kept the finances strictly under his own control, but I've been working here with him for some time and—except for the financial angle—I believe I know all there is to know about the way the office is run.'

'Bravo! I admire your spirit and I hope you succeed. But before we leave the subject may I offer just one small word of advice?'

'Well . . .' She gave him a cautious glance.

'I've seen too many owner-managers come to grief because they were determined to operate in isolation and were suspicious of getting external help. Will you promise me you won't join their ranks? I'd like to think you'd turn to me if you ever got really worried. I'd like to think we were friends, even after this rather disastrous start.'

Friends! She'd never thought of any man as a friend. She'd been romantically infatuated with Derek and he had done his best to use her for his own selfish ends. Father had bullied her and manipulated her. Robert was bidding fair to do the same. Was Bart Marchant different from the rest of the male sex? A man who really cared what happened to her? Suddenly she wanted to believe it.

'Philippa?' he prompted quietly.

A slow smile touched her lips. 'I don't make promises,' she said.

He sighed. 'I suppose I'll have to be content with that.'

She began to stack together the papers and folders on the desk and push them into drawers. This was the end of the matter, then. He would go in a moment or two. She was aware of a dragging feeling of regret somewhere in the region of her chest. She didn't want him to go . . . she wanted . . . she didn't know what she wanted. Just to get to know him better, perhaps.

Bart got to his feet. She waited for him to say goodbye, but instead he said, 'I like your honesty, Philippa. In fact, I like everything about you.' His eyes moved for a moment from her face to the soft swell of her breast as she sat at the desk, and then quickly back again, as if he regretted the momentary hint of sexual awareness.

'Now that we understand the situation, if I asked you again to have dinner with me, would I get a different answer from yesterday? I'd like to have the opportunity of proving that I'm not an insensitive clot.'

Philippa hesitated. It was a long time since she had been out with a man. But now she was free to do as she liked, to go out with anyone she wanted to, and it was a heady feeling. Bart Marchant had relinquished his role of trouble-shooter, so he must be asking her out simply because he wanted her company—and, of course, to ease his conscience.

And there was only cold pasta in the fridge waiting to be heated up!

'Thank you,' she said. 'I'd like that. So long as you don't intend to talk business.'

'This shall be an entirely personal occasion,' he promised gravely.

She wasn't sure how to take that but decided to ignore it. 'Would you like to come up to the flat and wait while I get changed?'

She led the way up the wide staircase, hoping he wouldn't notice that the stair carpet was distinctly threadbare. For a moment depression struck. How was she going to cope with everything—the house, the business? Was Robert right—was it going to be too much for her? *No*, she decided stubbornly, somehow she'd manage.

'My flat's on the second floor,' she told him as they climbed up. 'The first floor was my father's domain—there's nobody living there now. Sorry it's so far up.'

'Keeps you fit,' he said cheerfully. 'I must come and see you more often. Do you ever get right up to the top?'

'I haven't been up there for ages.' Suddenly Philippa felt slightly crazy. 'Do you want to lose another pound or two?' She looked up the twisting ascending stairs, narrower from this point upwards.

'I'm game if you are,' Bart chuckled. 'Lead on. How many floors are there? I've lost count.'

'Five in all, including the basement.' She switched on lights as she went. The bare bulbs threw a dim yellowish glow on the dusty uncarpeted stairs.

They reached the top floor and went into the front room, which was empty except for two old cabin trunks, thick with cobwebs. Father must have had them stored up here at some time and never mentioned it.

Bart walked across the creaky boards and stood at the window, looking down over the square. The rain had stopped and the wind had got up. It was almost dark now and the street lights shone gold through the bare branches of the trees, which waved and swayed as they were caught by sudden gusts.

'Super houses the Victorians built for themselves,' he mused. 'Even up here there's plenty of space. I suppose this was where the domestic staff had their quarters. Can you imagine the skivvies getting up at half-past five to creep down, shivering, to the cellar kitchens? Then they'd have to carry coal up to light all the fires, and then deliver hot water to the bedrooms. Up and down all those stairs!' He smiled wryly. 'There's a dark reverse-side to nostalgia.'

He was prowling round, poking at the walls, leaning to peer at the wainscoting. 'You'll have a bit of repair work to do up here, Philippa, if you're thinking of letting the rooms to students—isn't that what you said? And have you thought about the roof?' As he spoke the wind got through to the rafters, with an ominous whistling noise.

She sensed danger. This was the management consultant talking, no doubt totting up just how much it would cost to put the house in order. She winced as she imagined what the bill would be. 'The roof isn't my favourite subject for contemplation,' she said coolly, turning away to look down at one of the cobwebby trunks.

'Oh, dear, I've put my foot in it again. Sorry, Philippa, I didn't mean to interfere. Am I forgiven?' His voice came close to her ear as he put a friendly hand on her shoulder. She swung round, intending to pull away, and then she found she couldn't. The warmth of his fingers, resting on her shoulder, seemed to seep into her, travelling down her body, relaxing every part until she felt weak and dizzy.

Neither of them moved. In the dim light his dark blue eyes held an unmistakable question. She knew he wanted to kiss her—and that he was waiting for her to give the signal.

Philippa felt as if she were suspended in time and space. This was something she hadn't expected and she was confused by an urgency that shocked her. She *wanted* to feel his arms close round her, to feel his mouth on hers. Stop it, she warned herself. This is insane; you mustn't start anything with this stranger. Anyway, he was probably married.

She waited, unable to move, for his mouth to come down to hers, and when it did she almost fainted.

Her lips parted and she kissed him back with a passion that took her completely by surprise. Shamelessly she pressed herself against him, needing the intimate feeling of his strong body close to hers.

His kiss was deep and hungry. Not a flirtatious kiss but one that seemed to hold a yearning need. It went on and on until she could hardly breathe. Then she felt a long shudder pass through him and he took his mouth from hers and moved away. She put a hand on the window-frame to steady herself. Her cheeks were burning, her knees were rubbery.

Bart drew in an uneven breath. 'I promised this evening would be an entirely personal occasion, but please believe me when I say that I didn't have anything quite so personal as this in mind.' He slanted her a wry grin. 'Well, no more in mind than would be expected of any man who looked at you, Philippa. You're very beautiful.'

Strangely enough, she *did* believe him. He was civilised and mature—not the kind of man to pounce at the first opportunity.

She gave him a very small smile. 'I didn't exactly object, did I?'

He stuck his hands in his pockets, shaking his head slightly. 'Perhaps we've both been missing out on— er—certain aspects of living. I know I have.' His face was suddenly dark. 'My wife Paula walked out on me just about six months ago. The divorce finally came through last week.'

'Oh,' she said blankly. 'I didn't know.' Why should she know? The man was a stranger, and yet she had an odd feeling that she ought to know everything about him.

There was a silence which seemed to lengthen as their eyes met and held. Then Bart gave his shoulders a little shake. 'Let's go and have dinner.' He smiled and held out his hand.

She put her hand in his and as she felt the warm strength of his fingers enclosing hers she had a feeling of inevitability. Something important was beginning and she didn't know whether she could handle it.

She remembered Chloe's words about affairs: 'They're heavenly at the beginning.' Was that what she wanted—an affair with Bart? A few minutes ago she would have dismissed the idea with scorn. The last three years had shown her that she didn't need a man in her life. She'd been content behind the wall she had built for herself, and certainly none of the young men who had looked hopefully at the pretty secretary with the big grey eyes who sat behind the desk at the Albany Press had been given the slightest encouragement. But this man was different—older, confident, a man of the world. She had never met anyone quite like him and she felt out of her depth. And fascinated.

Bart looked back to her over his shoulder as they went down the dimly lit staircase. 'Careful here,' he warned, 'there's a bit of rough wood.' He held her hand a little tighter and chuckled. 'And I'm *not* speaking in a professional capacity.'

Philippa looked down. The wood was more than rough, it was rotten, and there was a jagged hole at the side of the tread. Perhaps, she thought, she should be worrying about having the repairs done to the house and not brooding about the effect a man's casual kiss was having on her.

Then, suddenly, she wasn't worrying about anything at all. There was a spring in her step and she felt more alive than she had done for years. The gloomy staircase seemed to be bathed in glittering light, and she was already trying to remember if she had a dress that was fit to wear for an evening date as she ran lightly down the stairs with her hand in Bart's.

'Welcome to my very own domain,' Philippa sang out as she led the way into her living-room. 'There's a good view over the square from here. On a fine day you can see the Warwick Road—except that you never can see it for cars. The traffic gets worse and worse every day.' She was gabbling, she knew, but it was as if a spring had been released inside her. She had a feeling she could fly up into the air. Calm yourself, you idiot, she ordered, you're not a teenager. Poise! Dignity, *if* you please.

Bart stood in the middle of the large room, looking round appreciatively at the cheerful chaos. Books piled on every flat surface, except for the ones that were occupied by compact discs. A deep chair with a crumpled orange linen cover pulled up in front of a TV set, the small sofa table beside it suggesting solitary meals. The carpet was not entirely innocent of crumbs, and the large black and white cat was curled up peacefully in a corner of the sofa.

Philippa plumped up cushions. 'Sorry the place is in such a mess. It's rather missed out on being cleaned lately. Do sit down.'

'I like it,' Bart said, lowering himself into the sofa beside the cat. 'It looks...'

'Homey?' Philippa pulled a wry face. 'That's the excuse I make for myself.' She addressed the sleeping cat. 'Come along, Portly, time for dinner. He's rather middle-aged,' she explained. 'Has to be encouraged to take exercise. I'm not quite sure how old he is. He came from next door. The people were moving abroad and poor old Portly was going to be—liquidated. So I took him in and renamed him Portly—for obvious reasons.'

Bart said, 'You're fond of animals? I believe you once had an ambition to be a vet.'

'Did Robert tell you that? It was just a crazy dream and my father soon talked me out of it.' For a moment the grey eyes were wistful.

Portly raised his head reluctantly and yawned, and Philippa reached for him, encountering Bart's hand as he tickled the cat under his silky white chin. As their fingers brushed Philippa's breath caught, and her eyes met Bart's and seemed unable to look away again.

For what seemed minutes they stared at each other. The man relaxed first. He leaned back against the cushions, smiling lazily, still tickling Portly's chin.

Philippa pulled herself together with an effort. 'Come *along*, Portly.' She grabbed the cat, who was happily snuggling up against Bart's knee to be fondled, and bore him off to the kitchen. 'Stupid animal,' she scolded. 'Yes, of course, you *would* need a new tin of food opening, wouldn't you?' She rummaged in a drawer for the tin-opener, reached into a cupboard for a tin of cat food and attacked it rather violently, while Portly—now sufficiently awake to scent that a meal was imminent—started to weave round her legs, mewing pitifully.

'I think you'd better let me do that, before you maim yourself.' Bart's quiet voice came from the kitchen doorway as Philippa struggled for the third time to pierce the top of a particularly resistant tin.

He took the tin from her, opened it in a few neat movements and handed it back.

'Thank you,' said Philippa, taking it, being careful to avoid touching his hand. She couldn't trust herself to touch him at the moment.

'You can see I lead a solitary existence,' he said. 'I'm expert with a tin-opener.'

Solitary existence! Not for long. A man like Bart Marchant would never be short of women jostling each other for the privilege of making his life comfortable. She felt a tweak of jealousy.

'You live alone?' she asked casually, spooning out cat meat into Portly's bowl, her head lowered.

'More or less.' He wandered back to his position by the door-frame. 'Since I came to live in the country I've had a succession of housekeepers, some tolerable, some frankly appalling. The dear old family retainer, the motherly type beloved of fiction, who makes wonderful beefsteak puddings and apple tarts, seems to be just that—fiction.' He shrugged. 'Mostly I eat out. Which is what I propose to do this evening, as you know. May I use your phone to book a table at my usual place—a rather nice country club not far from my home?'

'Of course. Where is your home, by the way?'

'It's rather in the middle of nowhere. An old farm-house about ten miles from here. The nearest bus route is a good twenty minutes' walk away and there are two buses a day into Stratford. Hence the house-keeper difficulty. I have to have someone who can drive a car and that usually means a younger woman—probably one with a failed marriage, looking out for a replacement, preferably well-heeled.' He shuddered expressively. 'There have been one or two rather dis-astrous—er—experiments.'

OK, she thought, I get the message. You've had a bad marriage and you don't intend to risk it again. It was probably the usual warning he gave to any woman with whom he had more than a passing ac-quaintance. Well, she supposed that was honest, at any rate.

'Not all women are searching for a man to keep them,' she said shortly. It would be a kind of dis-loyalty to let such a sexist remark go unchallenged. And she welcomed the opportunity to oppose him. Up in the attic she'd been in danger, for a brief moment, of imagining herself falling under his spell, which didn't accord at all with her new, independent self-image. 'There are ones who prefer to make their own way—on their own.'

The amusement in his eyes turned to a definite twinkle. 'Like you?'

'Like me,' she endorsed briefly. 'Now, would you like to make your phone call while I go and change? The only phone's down in the office.' She didn't vol-unteer any explanation for the fact that there was no extension in her flat.

He sketched a little bow as she walked past him to the bedroom. 'Certainly, ma'am. As you wish, ma'am.' His chuckle followed her as she closed the bedroom door.

CHAPTER FOUR

PHILIPPA stared at herself in her wardrobe mirror and was surprised that she looked much the same as usual after what had happened.

She struggled for some semblance of sanity. What *had* happened? A man had asked a girl for a date—nothing world-shaking about that. And his kiss—mere propinquity, that was all it was, nothing to get excited about. But there *had* been something more, she was sure of it. A recognition. That meeting of eyes had meant something—something that she wasn't prepared to face.

Forget it, she told herself, you're probably imagining things anyway. Just because Chloe had talked about having affairs, and quoted that bit about 'one day you'll see a stranger...'

That was how it had happened with Derek. That sudden feeling of togetherness—of rightness—and look where that had led! She wasn't going to make that mistake again.

She slid open the wardrobe door and took out the violet jersey dress which was the only new thing she'd bought for months. It hadn't been expensive but she had loved it from the first moment she'd set eyes on it in the window of a small boutique in the shopping mall. She hadn't really needed—or been able to afford—a new dress, but she had been tempted and fallen. It had hung in the wardrobe under its plastic cover ever since, unworn, waiting for an excuse to wear it.

Pulling off her skirt and blouse, she swilled her face, cleaned her teeth, brushed her hair until it curved like black satin into her neck, and smoothed on a light touch of eye-shadow in a darker shade than her dress, and a gloss of pink lipstick. Then she slipped the dress over her head and fitted in the pair of pearl stud earrings that had been her mother's. Yes, the dress fitted beautifully, moulding her small, firm breasts, clinging in all the right places and swinging out into soft flutes round her knees. She passed her hands slowly down over the curves of her body and a tremor ran through her. Again she heard Chloe's words: 'You don't intend to live like a nun for the rest of your life, I take it.'

She stared at her reflection in the long mirror as if her sister were standing there. 'All right, Sis, perhaps I don't, but this is much too quick, and I'd have to be sure this time.'

A final glance in the mirror gave her confidence—she saw a cool girl, very much her own mistress. She was going to enjoy the evening, she promised herself. Bart was a sophisticated, interesting man and the most important thing was that he wanted her company for its own sake and not for any selfish reason. She was almost sure he wasn't the kind of man who would expect repayment in his bed for a dinner-date. If she was wrong and that was what he had in mind he was going to be disappointed.

When she returned to the living-room Bart was standing at the far end of the room, examining a CD record. He treated her to an appreciative inspection. 'You look charming, Philippa,' he said.

'Thank you.' She gave him a composed little smile. Not for the world would she let him think she was trying to start a flirtation with him.

'I like your choice of records too. Mozart—Schubert—they seem to reflect your personality. Do I take it you're not a pop addict?'

'Not really.' Philippa tried to think of something amusing to say but nothing came. Just looking at the man standing there, the glow from the overhead light emphasising the faint waves in his teak-brown hair, made her mouth go dry. She picked up a record and bent over it, because she was sure her cheeks were a give-away. 'My mother was a pianist,' she said. 'I never knew her—she died when I was born—but I think I must have inherited her love for classical music. Somehow I never got into pop and discos.'

Bart was watching her face with a curious expression in his dark blue eyes, and she went on quickly, 'The CD player was a Christmas present to myself, and I collect as many of the old recordings that are being re-mastered I can afford. This is a super one of the Elgar, played by the sixteen-year-old Yehudi Menuhin. Fantastic!'

'Yes, I've got that one—it's marvellous!' he agreed enthusiastically. 'Have you come across the early Callas set? I must lend it to you, you'd love it.'

They talked music happily on the way out of the house and Philippa found herself feeling more and more at ease with Bart. The car was a joy to drive in—it purred through the town and once out into the country it gobbled up the miles almost languidly. It was, Philippa thought, exactly the kind of car that Bart would choose to drive—powerful, polished, sophisticated. She laid her head back against the soft leather and watched the white cone of headlights and listened dreamily to the tape that was filling the car with music that seemed to her a perfect complement to the occasion.

She turned her head. 'What is it?'

'Delius, *On hearing the first cuckoo in spring*. Know it?'

'No, but I love it. It's super to think that spring's just round the corner. It's my favourite time of the year, it always seems more like the beginning of things than New Year's Day, somehow.' And this spring was going to be the best ever, for she was free. Free to live her life as she wanted to.

She saw him nod in a satisfied kind of way. He's analysing me, she thought; it's probably second nature with him to probe into the personality of his clients. But it didn't seem to matter, and anyway she wasn't a client.

Very soon they were turning into a drive between tall gateposts and pulling up beside several other cars in the forecourt of an enormous old building that seemed to spread out in all directions, with wings and gables and long mullioned windows from which light shone whitely and welcomingly across the darkness of the gravel and into the dense stand of tall conifers behind it.

'Once what was known as a gentleman's residence,' Bart announced as he got out of the car and came round to open the door for Philippa. 'They haven't spoilt it inside: it has "atmosphere".' He held out his hand and eased her gently out of the low seat, and she felt curiously content and almost could have purred like Portly.

Inside, as he had promised, the house still had the feeling of a gracious home, with wood panelling, imposing crystal chandeliers, gracefully curving staircase, and a muted atmosphere of luxury and ease. Bart was obviously a valued member of the club and subtly deferred to by the staff. A tubby little man with a red face and formidable moustache greeted them and took Philippa's coat, and they were escorted to a corner table in the softly lit dining-room, where tempting smells hung lightly in the air, and waiters glided between the tables that were already occupied.

'OK?' Bart smiled across the table at Philippa as a white-jacketed waiter appeared with huge menu cards.

Philippa took the card. Always, when she had dined out with Derek, he had never consulted her. She had been so stupidly besotted with him that she'd liked that—liked what she had thought of as his masterful approach. Much later, when she'd come to her senses, she had realised that he hadn't cared what she ate, he was weighing up the cost against the possible advantage of dining at a restaurant where he might make business contacts. The thought of giving his fiancée a treat had never entered his head. She was merely a decoration.

But this evening all was different. She could hold up her head—she was free to choose. And independent young women chose for themselves.

'The table d'hôte looks fine to me,' she said.

The waiter flourished his pencil over its pad. 'Madam will have soup? Hors d'ouevres? *Crudités*?'

Philippa enjoyed going through the items, picking out the ones she fancied—deciding for herself. A trivial thing, but it was a small sign of how the new Philippa was shaping up. When they had both ordered and Bart had had a heart-to-heart with the wine waiter, he leaned back in his chair and said, 'I do like a girl who knows her own mind. The ones who sigh, "Oh, darling, you order for me," are rather a bore.'

Philippa was torn between relishing the compliment and fighting back a niggling little feeling of something alarmingly like jealousy when she thought of all the girls he took out to dinner. The girls who called him 'darling'.

The niggle disappeared as dinner went on and Bart was obviously enjoying her company and giving her his full attention. He put himself out to amuse her, and his long account of his recent visit to Mexico and how he had come by a donkey and—after a lengthy battle of wills with the said donkey—had finally had to admit defeat made her laugh so much that she nearly choked on a sliver of carrot from the *crudités*.

The duck *à l'orange* was delicious, definitely a change from fish fingers and frozen peas, which had been Philippa's staple diet for the past few days. Her glass kept on being filled up with the delicate *rosé* wine. She sighed as she spooned up the final trickle of luscious pineapple ice-cream confection. 'That was really lovely.'

Bart smiled warmly across the table at her. 'Lovely!' he echoed, and her cheeks were warm as she knew he wasn't referring to the meal.

He said, 'Let's go back to my house and Mrs McLeod will make us coffee. After the wine I need a cup or two of black coffee before I drive you home. Mrs McLeod is my latest housekeeper, by the way, and I have high hopes of her.'

Philippa didn't hesitate. 'I'd love to come,' she said simply and was rewarded by a pleased smile. A smile that said they both knew the score and would play the game by the rules.

Nothing had happened to make her believe that he intended to pounce on her the moment they were alone. No, he just wasn't that kind of man, he was of a different order entirely. He had far too much subtlety to need the leer, the pressure of thigh against thigh, the doubtful joke. He didn't flaunt his sexuality but it was there all the time, under the surface, like a damped-down fire, sending little *frissons* of excitement through her body when their eyes met, when he touched her briefly, helping her on with her coat.

The short drive took them deep into the darkness of the Warwickshire countryside, through a maze of twisty narrow roads that were unfamiliar to Philippa. Eventually they passed down a lane that was little more than a field track and drew up outside a long, low cottage almost hidden in evergreen shrubs and low-growing trees.

'This was my godmother's home,' Bart said as they got out of the car. 'She was an artist and she liked seclusion. I used to stay with her in the school holidays when my parents were abroad—my father was in the diplomatic service before he retired and they were away a good deal. My godmother was a lovely lady and I adored her; we had some wonderful times together here. When she died last year she left me the cottage, and my first thought was that I wanted to live here. I haven't regretted it for a moment.'

As they reached the front door it opened wide, letting light stream out from the hall and disclosing a tall thin woman in a dark dress. 'I heard the car, Mr Marchant,' she announced in a broad Scots accent.

'I thought ye'll be wanting some coffee.' She eyed Philippa severely as Bart ushered her into the hall.

'And how right you were, Mrs McLeod. Come in, Philippa. This is my new housekeeper, Mrs McLeod, who makes marvellous coffee and no doubt has other culinary accomplishments which I have yet to discover.' He beamed at the woman, whose thin face creased into a smile. The man was a real charmer, Philippa thought in amusement. He's got her on his side already.

Bart led the way into a long, low living-room with a cheerful log fire burning at one end.

'It's perfect.' Philippa sighed with appreciation, looking round at the solid oak furniture, the plain linen covers on the chairs and sofas, the thick ceiling beams. 'Just how a country cottage should look.'

Bart gave her an appreciative grin. 'I agree. I think old houses should have their own personality preserved. I haven't changed a thing since Tilly—that's my godmother—died. Somehow there was so much of her left here that I couldn't bear to.'

They settled down, one each side of the fire, with a low table between them, and drank the excellent coffee Mrs McLeod produced, and crunched little coconut biscuits, and Bart talked about the holidays he had spent at the cottage, and how his godmother had taken him on long tramps in the countryside when he was a boy home from school.

'It doesn't sound a very thrilling way to spend school holidays,' he mused. 'But I was never much of a one for sports or motor racing and so on. Tilly was a real countrywoman; she knew every fox-hole, every hedge that harboured hedgehogs. And there were otters living in a hollow tree by the river. She had made a sort of hide and we watched them for hours.' In the glow from the fire his dark blue eyes shone with a remembered pleasure.

Philippa leaned back and sipped her coffee and watched him with a lazy feeling of happiness such as she couldn't remember ever feeling before. It was all so right. *He* was so right, so different from any other man she'd ever had anything to do with. She just knew that they were at the beginning of something that would stretch into the future. That somehow they would be together.

'If you're not too bored there's another childhood memory you might be interested in—which would explain my enthusiasm when I very presumptuously barged into your printing shop earlier on. I had an illness when I was a kid—and I had to stay in bed for quite a time. Tilly was marvellous, she brought me books and puzzles and things to amuse me, among which was an old toy printing set she'd had herself as a child. You fixed little rubbery type into a wooden block with grooves in it, and inked it on a pad and then pressed it on to a sheet of paper and—eureka! Your very own words appeared in print, rocky spelling and all. It seemed like magic, and from that moment I was hooked on printing. Still am. My eyes light up when I see a press, especially an old one like the Albion I saw in your printing shop. Does that explain anything?' He took another coconut biscuit from the plate and added with a grin, 'I can see my new "treasure" is going to be bad for my waistline.'

He leaned his head back comfortably. 'Now, tell me how your printing business came into being. I don't intend to interfere, I'm just interested, that's all. Is it a family firm?'

Philippa was no longer on the defensive about his trouble-shooter brief from Robert, and the picture of him being ill in bed when he was a little boy had touched a chord inside her somewhere. She said, 'My father bought the house in Albany Square, together with the printing business, when he retired.' There was no need to go into all the details of the failure of the family hardware firm, was there? Especially as Robert had evidently not told Bart about it.

'My father was a bit of a workaholic,' she went on. 'Retirement didn't suit him and he wanted something to keep him busy and interested. He worked very hard on it for three years, but then his health started to fail and the business went downhill a bit. However, I intend to remedy that quite soon,' she added as an afterthought. She couldn't let him guess that her interest in the business had this evening suffered a partial eclipse by something more—personal, as Bart had called it.

'And how long were you working with your father?'

'Nearly three years. Since I left commercial college.'

He didn't ask her any more questions. He just nodded. 'Well, I wish you luck for the future.'

He was silent for a time as if he was weighing something up. Then he said casually, 'I'll probably come across your brother from time to time, so I'll be able to enquire how you're making out.'

From time to time! He'd enquire about her now and again if he *happened* to meet Robert! Philippa felt as if she'd been punched in the stomach. She hadn't realised how much she'd been counting on his wanting to continue their relationship. But he could hardly make it plainer that this evening was a one-off date. He'd asked her out to dinner because he felt a little guilty about the high-handed way he'd behaved. It had been a duty invitation and he'd probably been bored with her on closer acquaintance.

Or was it because she'd responded too enthusiastically to his kiss up there in the attic? Had he been lumping her together with the predatory housekeepers? She felt hot all over at the idea.

It was like a game, and she was a raw beginner. She was out of her depth with a man like this. Chloe would have known how to cope, she thought dispiritedly. Well, there was nothing she could do about it. If he didn't want to see her again then he didn't; what did it matter to her?

She got to her feet and said with a false, brilliant smile, 'I must be getting home. Busy day tomorrow. It's a shame to take you out again—perhaps you could phone for a taxi?'

Bart's eyebrows rose and he looked rather hard at her. 'I didn't hear that remark. Of course I shall drive you back. Come along.'

He piloted her masterfully out to the car. He was probably quite glad to get rid of her, she thought gloomily. Certainly he drove very fast indeed and didn't attempt to make conversation. Philippa sat in silence, almost unbearably aware of the man beside her, of the strong slender fingers resting on the steering-wheel, of the slight movement of his thighs as his feet controlled the pedals. Would he think it was expected of him to kiss her goodnight? She couldn't bear that—not a casual kiss that meant nothing. Almost a habit-kiss.

The car pulled up outside number sixteen Albany Square and Bart turned to her, sliding his arm along the back of her seat. 'Philippa...'

She pretended not to hear. Releasing her seatbelt, she felt for the door-handle, praying that the door wasn't locked. It wasn't, and she slipped out quickly.

'Don't bother getting out,' she said brightly as Bart started to open his door. 'I've got my key all ready.' She dangled it on its ring. 'Thank you so much for the lovely dinner, I did enjoy it. Goodnight—Bart.'

She ran up the steps and, after a second's fumbling, managed to fit the key into the lock. Then she turned and looked down. Bart was still sitting behind the wheel of the car, looking up at her, the golden light from the street lamp shining on his strong face, making it all shadows and angles. She couldn't make out his expression.

She waved gaily, let herself in, and closed the door.

She went into the office without turning on the light. Her knees were shaking and she sank down into a chair near the door. She could hear the Jaguar panting softly outside. He was still there, and for a moment all sorts of wild thoughts rushed through her head. What would she do if he came after her? If the front doorbell rang? She held her breath, listening intently in the darkened office. Then, from outside the window, came an impatient roar, fading as the car drove away along the service road. There was something final about the silence that followed.

She had kept her pride. She had been as casual as he had been himself. She didn't suppose she would be seeing Bart Marchant again.

With a small pain in the region of her heart, Philippa went very slowly up to bed.

He wouldn't phone, of course he wouldn't, Philippa told herself, sitting at her desk next morning. It was stupid to allow herself to think he might. She had impressed that fact on her mind when she had found herself waking at short intervals in the night, recalling every detail of the dinner-date and the unsatisfactory ending to it.

A fine way for a modern, self-confident young woman to behave, she had scolded herself. Chloe wouldn't have scuttled away defensively like a scared rabbit—by the middle of the night Philippa had got everything out of proportion.

What *would* Chloe have done? she wondered now as she tackled the morning post. Invited Bart in for yet another coffee? And then...?

Stop it, she told herself. There were pressing problems to deal with that didn't include Bart Marchant.

She began to slit open envelopes which seemed to contain little else than bills, and glossy brochures offering loans and credit. The latter she threw into the waste-basket, tempting though they might appear. She couldn't risk taking on more debts on top of the overdraft. Or could she? For the sake of updating the printing presses to attract more business and make the company's future more secure?

A frown puckered her forehead. This was the kind of decision that company managers had to make all the time and she was in the managerial seat now. All of a sudden the responsibility weighed heavily on her. Bart would tell her what was best for the firm without blinking an eyelid. Oh, forget Bart Marchant, she instructed herself crossly; she wasn't going crawling back to him for help after the show of self-reliance she had put on.

She could hear the familiar clatter of the printing presses below. Ernie would be finishing the order for Forrester's, a firm which was soon to open a new wine-bar in the town and which was planning a door-to-door distribution of leaflets. They had beaten her down over the price, but hopefully they would pay cash on delivery. That was the usual arrangement with new customers and they had agreed.

She turned the pages of the order-book. There were one or two orders for bits and pieces advertising shops and services. They would be enclosed with the local free papers but the profit on them hardly paid for the paper they were printed on. There was a small order for wedding stationery and another for business cards, but after that—nothing. Philippa forced back a rising feeling of panic. Surely something would come in soon to boost the cash flow. But if it didn't——

The front doorbell rang and she hurried into the hall. A smiling girl stood on the step holding a cellophane-swathed bunch of early spring flowers tied by an enormous bow of pale blue ribbon.

'Miss Price?' The girl held out the sheaf and Philippa took it, her insides fluttering. Bart, she thought. Surely nobody else would send her flowers?

'Thank you.' She watched the girl trip down the steps to the bright little van and wave before she drove off. Then she carried the flowers into the office and put them very gently down on the desk.

There was a tiny envelope attached to the blue bow. Her hands were shaking as she opened it and took out the card inside. The words on the card, written in a firm hand that could only be his, read,

To remind you that spring really is on the way and to thank you for last evening. See you soon. Bart.

Tenderly Philippa unwrapped the sheaf of flowers and held them in her arms. Daffodils, great golden trumpets. Narcissi, white and fragrant with delicate orange centres. Shaggy double tulips, pink and crimson. She laid her cheek against the cool, smooth dampness of the petals, and blinked back her tears. Nobody had ever sent her flowers before. Even when they were engaged, Derek had never given her flowers.

She carried the sheaf to the kitchen and found vases in the back of a cupboard. The flowers filled three vases. The daffodils she put on her desk in the office and the other two vases she carried up to her flat. They transformed the living-room, filling it with the fresh, fragrant promise of spring, lightening the gloom of the morning as they were lightening the gloom in Philippa's heart. Something wonderful was happening, she knew it was. 'See you soon,' he had written. He didn't need to say that if he didn't mean it, did he? Philippa returned to her desk with new optimism.

After a week the optimism was beginning to wear thin. Bart hadn't been in touch again; she'd heard nothing from him. The order from Forrester's had been completed and delivered but the promised payment hadn't been received, and Philippa was trying to nerve herself to get tough with them.

And then, at half-past eleven on Friday morning, she answered the bell to find Bart standing on the top step, a brown paper parcel in his hand and a heart-stopping smile on his mouth.

'Hello, Philippa, how are you?'

Philippa's heart lurched and began a heavy thudding. 'Oh, hello,' she managed. 'I'm fine, how are you?' There was more than a touch of arrogance about him today. He was wearing a dark business suit but the colourful flamboyance of his tie suggested a breezy, adventurous side to him. He looked—fabulous. So big, so forceful, so very, very masculine.

'Hungry. I left Carlisle this morning before my hotel had begun to think about serving breakfast, and motorway service-station cafés looked unappealing. How about making me a sandwich before I set out for Birmingham? Or are you too busy?'

'No, of course not, I was just thinking of lunch myself.' Little trickles of excitement were running through her like wine. 'Come up to the flat.'

The shabby hall was full of light and colour because he was there. She led the way upstairs, talking in a high, 'social' voice. 'Did you manage to find somewhere to park? It gets more and more difficult.'

'I've left the car at my garage,' he said, following her up. 'It needed a small adjustment to the engine—they're attending to it before I have to drive back to Birmingham.'

They had reached the second floor by now and Philippa turned to him. 'You're driving to Birmingham and you had to come all this way round to have your car done? How maddening for you!' That was an inane remark. She wished she could think of something witty and amusing to say. As she looked up and met the brilliant blue eyes looking down at her her breathing was shallow and fast—but perhaps that could be put down to hurrying up all those stairs.

'No,' Bart said, blue eyes twinkling. 'I came "all this way round" because I wanted to see you, Philippa.' His tone was definitely teasing.

'What a charming thought!' Just the right touch of mockery in her voice—Chloe would have been proud of her. 'And thank you so much for the flowers—they're beautiful, they really brought a touch of spring to the house. Look, there are still some tulips left. Do switch on the fire and sit down while I rustle up some food.'

Breathing fast, she escaped into the kitchen. Here she took a loaf from the cupboard, a tub of margarine and a slab of cheese from the fridge and rather feverishly began to make sandwiches. Was it true, then—was he 'courting' her, if you could call it that in these uninhibited days? Bart wasn't the kind of man to make a crude pass at a girl; he would take his time. But his look, his tone, his words, the flowers, all told her. Bart was experienced, worldly, sophisticated, and he had made it quite plain that he didn't have another marriage in mind. So what *did* he have in mind? A quick fling? A vague arrangement convenient to them both? Or was this the beginning of an affair—a semi-permanent relationship such as Chloe enthused over? If only she knew!

She found that she had cut a plateful of cheese sandwiches without noticing. The kettle was boiling and she made two mugs of instant coffee, arranged all that was left of yesterday's lettuce in a dish, piled gingerbread biscuits in another dish, put the whole lot on a tray and carried it to the living-room.

Bart was on his feet in an instant, taking the tray from her. 'This looks tempting—I'm positively slavering.'

Philippa had intended to put the tray on the low table beside her chair, so that he would sit in the chair opposite, but he had had other ideas. Two bars of the electric fire were glowing and he had made himself at home—pulling the sofa up to the fire, with the low table in front of it.

He put the tray on the table and sat down, patting the place beside him on the sofa. 'This is cosy. Don't watch while I make a pig of myself.' He helped himself to a sandwich and munched enthusiastically.

It was a two-seater sofa and Philippa began to feel much too aware of Bart's body so close to her. She was conscious of the smell of him, a clean masculine outdoor smell like heather or peat. Funny, really, when he wasn't an outdoor type. Or perhaps he was. Perhaps he was an enthusiastic gardener in his spare time or a dedicated jogger.

A picture of Bart in shorts and vest, pounding the Warwickshire country lanes, gave her a curious little tweak behind her ribs and she moved a few inches further away and said, 'Did you have a good trip?'

His mouth curved into his twisty little smile. 'So-so. I've been trying to sort out the mess that a knitwear company has got itself into. They make beautiful garments but haven't a clue how to market them. I think I've helped—I hope so.'

She nodded in silence. Reference to his job of saving ailing and inefficient companies was too close to home to be comfortable.

She glanced at him and saw the quirk of his lips, informing her that he was following her thoughts with embarrassing accuracy.

'But enough of work,' he said. 'It's good to see you again, Philippa. I've thought about you.'

Oh, and I've thought about you, too. But she couldn't say it, and she couldn't think of anything else to say. In her fantasies at night she had been relaxed and easy with him. They had laughed together, teased each other. But, now that he was actually sitting here beside her, her mouth was dry and she was stiff with self-consciousness.

Bart was making short work of the cheese sandwiches. 'I'm being horribly greedy,' he confessed. 'Have I left enough for you?'

'Plenty. I'm always careful about cheese sandwiches—too many calories.'

He leaned back in the corner of the sofa, his blue eyes creased into amusement. '*You* don't have to watch your figure—it's quite delightful.'

She could feel his gaze moving down from her eyes to rest on the swell of her breast under her white silky blouse. 'Which reminds me,' he went on, 'I've got something for you.' He reached down beside the sofa and brought up a brown paper parcel.

'For you,' he smiled, offering it to her. 'Open it, I want to see what you think.'

Philippa fumbled with the Sellotape fastening the parcel, her hands unsteady. 'It's like Christmas,' she said with awful brightness as the paper finally tore apart. Inside the parcel, swathed in tissue, was the most beautiful silky shawl—the palest dove-grey with small motifs of violets scattered here and there over it.

'I thought it would suit you,' Bart said. 'The grey matches your eyes.'

Confused, Philippa took refuge in facetiousness. 'And the violets match my character—is that what you thought? A shrinking violet?'

He didn't smile. He said slowly, 'I'm not sure. I've been wondering about you, Philippa.'

There was a little silence, then he said, 'Do you like it—is it wearable?' His eyes searched hers anxiously.

'*Wearable*? It's—it's heaven,' Philippa breathed. 'But——'

'Now don't say "You shouldn't have" or anything like that,' he said hastily. 'I'm well aware that I haven't qualified to buy you clothes, and it may seem—presumptuous. As a matter of fact it was a gift from a grateful client. The knitwear company I told you about asked me to accept it before I left—for my wife or girlfriend. As you know, I don't have a wife any longer, so perhaps you would consider yourself in the second category.'

Philippa wondered briefly just how many females there were in the second category. Never mind, he had brought the shawl to her, not to one of the others. Her fingers stroked the sleek, supple material. 'It's beautiful,' she said softly. 'Thank you very much.'

The dark blue eyes were fixed on her with a look that was almost puzzled. Then he said, 'Does it merit a thank-you kiss?'

Before she had time to think she reached up and put her lips softly to his cheek. He turned his head quickly so that his mouth closed on hers. He didn't touch her with his hands, but for a long, dizzy moment his mouth pressed hard against hers, his tongue flicking along her lips, sending shafts of delight down her spine, before he drew away.

He was breathing unevenly. 'You're very tempting, Philippa,' he said huskily, 'and right now I want to take you in my arms and kiss you properly. And perhaps . . .'

He shook his shoulders, took a final gulp of coffee and stood up. 'I must remove myself from temptation and remind myself that I've got an appointment in Birmingham at two o'clock, woe is me! Thank you again for the lunch. It's been delightful. Sorry it's been such a rush.'

She went downstairs with him, hanging on to the banisters because her legs felt curiously unsteady. He didn't pause on the step. 'See you soon.' He touched her shoulder lightly and was away, striding down the road.

She watched him reach the corner. A pale early-spring sun had come out and was lighting up the faint waves in his teak-brown hair. He was so tall and lithe. He looked—marvellous. He turned and lifted a hand in salute and she waved back.

She went in and closed the door and leaned back against it. What happens now? she thought dizzily. The next move must come from Bart and she shook inside as she knew what it must surely be. It really was the beginning of an affair after all. How was she going to handle it—and was she sure she wanted to go along that path? She was getting on to a roller-coaster and she didn't know where it would end up. There was only one thing she was sure about—the way her body reacted to Bart's. There was no doubt whatever about that!

She went back upstairs to clear away the lunch things and brood lovingly over the shawl he had brought her. 'I thought it would suit you,' he'd said. 'The grey matches your eyes.' Sighing happily, she carried it into the bedroom and draped it round her shoulders, surveying herself from all angles, then hugging it close to her body, savouring the fact that something new and exciting was happening to her for the first time in years. Finally she wrapped the shawl in its tissue and placed it carefully away in a drawer before she managed to drag herself back to earth to tackle the afternoon work-load.

Robert phoned almost as soon as she got back to the office. 'Hello, Pippa? Sorry I haven't been in touch—business trip to London. By the way, how did you get on with my friend, Bart Marchant?'

Robert was all sweetness and light today. He obviously thought he'd pulled a master-stroke in enlisting Bart to persuade her she should give up the business.

Philippa thought quickly. 'Oh, we got on very well,' she said lightly. 'He's a charming man.'

'Good—good. And you think he'll be able to help you to sort things out?' She recognised the quizzing note in Robert's voice, but she wasn't going to satisfy his curiosity.

'Oh, I'm sure he will.'

'Good,' Robert said again. He sounded definitely puzzled now. He wouldn't have been expecting that kind of enthusiastic response from her after the way she'd received his previous offer. 'Well, I expect I'll be running into Bart soon. We'll have a chat about your—er—difficulties.'

'Oh, yes?' Philippa said vaguely. 'How are Edith and the boys?'

This time it was Philippa who said goodbye and hung up. She sat looking down at the desk thoughtfully. She hadn't exactly lied to Robert but the conversation had brought it home to her that it was going to be difficult to keep her private self and her business self apart. Somehow, though, she was determined to do it, to succeed on her own.

Perhaps, much later on, if she and Bart were—were—partners, she could turn to him for advice. She wouldn't have to take it if she didn't want to. He had made it clear that he didn't intend to interfere in her business affairs. Any relationship she might have with Bart would leave her completely independent.

She pulled her chair up to the desk and drew the account books towards her. The end of the business year was looming close and with it the necessity of getting the figures sorted out for income tax. She picked up her Biro and tried hard to dismiss thoughts of Bart from her mind.

CHAPTER FIVE

THE effort to put Bart out of her mind didn't last long. Half an hour later the telephone rang and his deep voice came over the wire. 'Philippa?'

Her hand tightened on the receiver and her stomach lurched. Heavens, she thought, I only have to hear his voice . . .

'I've just got back to the office. Look, I can't stay more than two seconds, I've got a client waiting. I've come by a couple of tickets for Stratford for this evening—how about it? Can you make it at such short notice? I don't even know what the play is but we could chance it. It'll be a Shakespeare, of course.'

The figures in the accounts book swam before Philippa's eyes. 'Yes, I'd love to,' she said, not caring how eager she sounded.

'Splendid. I'll pick you up about six, then. 'Bye, darling.'

Darling! He'd called her darling. And she would see him again this evening—soon. She wanted to burst into song, or do a crazy dance round the room. Instead she closed the account books and got to her feet. She must wash her hair and make sure the violet dress was as good as she could make it. It would have been nice to dash out to the shops and splash out on something new, but there wasn't time. And anyway, the shawl would make any dress look good. It was going to be a wonderful evening, she thought, feeling a thrill right down to her toes. It would be the beginning of something momentous, she was almost sure. And if Bart had set his heart against another permanent commitment then she would have to settle for less. That was the way modern career-women managed their love-lives, and she was a modern career-woman. The only trouble was, she didn't really feel like one yet.

Philippa was to remember that evening for a long, long time to come. The play was *Othello*, but even that grim tragedy couldn't dampen her spirits as she sat beside Bart in the front row of the dress circle at the Royal Shakespeare Theatre. It was an intoxicating feeling to have as her escort the man who was, at least in her eyes, the best-looking, most distinguished man in the theatre that night. In the crush-room, during the interval, she saw how the eyes of other women rested on him as he made his way back to her through the crowd, balancing their drinks expertly. In the theatre restaurant, at the end of the performance, she felt a warm glow enveloping her dizzily when she met his eyes across the table as they ate a delicious grill and salad. It was as if there were only the two of them in the whole busy room.

'A good performance, I thought,' Bart said. 'How did you like it?'

'I enjoyed every minute of it. I haven't been here since we were brought in a school party to see *As You Like It*. We were right up in the gods and I was stuck behind a pillar.'

He laughed. How white his teeth were, how glinting blue his eyes! '*As You Like It*? Quite a step from there to the dark brooding passion of the Moor.'

She felt suddenly at ease with him—enough to tease him. 'Do I detect a hint of cynicism?'

'About dark, brooding passion?' His mouth turned down at the corners. 'Not exactly my cup of tea. Anyway, the bloke was rather an idiot to kill the girl who obviously doted on him.'

She nodded thoughtfully. 'She was pretty idiotic too, wasn't she, trusting so blindly in his love for her, expecting that he felt the same way?'

'Yes,' he said slowly, 'Trust, that's what cements a relationship. Not sex, not love even. Without trust it all falls apart. And if the trust is betrayed...'

Philippa looked up from chasing a piece of gateau round her plate. The conversation was getting into deep water and she intended to bring it safely back, but the light words died on her lips as she saw Bart's bent head, his mouth taut with bitterness, and she knew he wasn't thinking about her at all.

But in a moment or two he looked up across the table at her. 'Memories, memories!' he said wryly. 'No doubt you have them too. Are they good ones, or is that an unpardonable question?'

'None that I want to remember.' Memories of Derek seemed very remote now. 'Does that answer your question?'

Surprisingly, he laughed aloud. 'You *do* sound fierce, Philippa. Thank you for telling me. It seems we have more than Mozart and Schubert in common.' Their eyes met and held, and again there was that message she had seen up in the attic that first day. She looked away, confused.

Bart was selecting a credit card from his wallet as the waiter approached and she stole a glance at his face, but it told her nothing. He looked as calm and controlled now as he always looked. Would he look as calm as that when he made love? she wondered, and shivered inwardly as she contemplated the remainder of the evening. It would be late by the time they got back to Albany Square. If she invited him in, would that be a signal to him . . . ?

'Ready, Philippa?' He came round and pulled back her chair. 'I'm glad you wore my gift,' he smiled, giving her a little hug as he draped the shawl round her shoulders. 'It looks good on you. I knew it would.'

'It would look good on anyone,' she returned rather awkwardly as they left the restaurant, wishing she had had more practice in returning compliments gracefully.

'I'll leave you to wait here while I get the car,' Bart said as they reached the theatre entrance hall.

Philippa's mouth drooped. She had been looking forward to the walk along the riverbank to the car park, with the dark water flowing softly beside them and perhaps a swan gliding past. 'I could come with you.' She saw his eyes travel from the hem of the violet jersey dress down her legs in their sheer stockings to her thin court shoes, and he shook his head firmly. 'No, you stay in the warm. I won't be long.'

Once in the car, it became obvious that the drive would not encourage conversation. The traffic on the Stratford-Leamington road was incessant, and Philippa leaned back against the Jaguar's luxuriously cushioned seat and closed her eyes against the white glare of dipped headlights and tried not to think ahead.

'Comfy?' Bart flicked her a glance.

'Um—yes, thanks, very comfy.' She longed to wriggle up against him, but that wasn't her style— yet. Perhaps after tonight things would be different and she would be able to give in to this constant yearning to be close to him, to touch him. She melted inside at the prospect.

All too soon the Jaguar drew up in the only vacant parking-space near number sixteen Albany Square. 'That was a bit of luck,' Bart said.

So he *did* intend to come in with her. He came round and opened the car door and helped her out. They walked up the steps together to the front door. Philippa's hands shook as she fumbled in her bag for her key and pushed it into the lock, turning on the porch light from the outside switch.

Bart opened the door and glanced inside, at the steep flight of stairs receding into the gloom at the end of the hall. 'You know, I don't like to think of you being here at night all on your own, Philippa,' he said.

Portly, the black and white cat, came lolloping heavily down the stairs, having heard the door open. Philippa picked him up and buried her face in his soft fur. 'I'm not alone—see? My protector.' She lifted up the cat's chin to demonstrate, and led the way upstairs.

In the living-room the sofa was still pulled up in front of the fire, where Bart had put it at lunchtime. He leaned down and switched on the electric fire, rubbing his hands together. 'Brrh! It's too cold for you in here. You should have central heating put in, you know.'

Philippa laughed. 'In this house? Have you counted the number of rooms? When I make my first million I'll consider it. Anyway, I don't feel the cold.' It was a lie, but it was good to think that he cared about her comfort, worried about her safety. 'Would you like coffee—or a drink?'

'A very small whisky, if you can manage it.' He held up two fingers to demonstrate the amount.

Philippa had included a bottle of whisky in her weekly shopping list, as a sort of hostage to fortune. She poured him out a small glass now, and an even smaller amount for herself, doctoring it with plenty of water. As she handed him his glass their fingers brushed together and she was suddenly shaken right down to her toes.

She subsided into a corner of the sofa, her knees like stretched elastic, waiting for what would happen next. She wished he would sit down, touch her hand, anything to lead up to what he was going to say in a way that would break the tension hanging between them. The ache to feel his arms round her was painful. But he didn't sit down. He stood with his back to the fire—in the way Robert usually stood, she thought, and she almost giggled. Robert would be horrified when he knew the result of sending his 'colleague' to persuade her to give up her business.

'Philippa——' Bart began and, for the first time, he looked uncertain of himself. 'Philippa—I've got a proposition to put to you.'

Her stomach did a somersault. This was it, then. From now on she would be the new Philippa, the modern career-girl, running her own business, having an affair with a fabulously attractive man.

'Proposition?' she echoed as casually as she could.

He stuck both hands in his pockets, and looked down at the hearthrug. 'I've thought about this a lot and I wanted to say it before, but I didn't want to rush you. We're friends now, aren't we, so I'll pluck up my courage?'

Philippa passed her tongue over her dry lips, saying nothing. *Why* didn't he sit down beside her?

'I know you're an independent young lady, and you told me you didn't want any interference from anyone in your business, but I have to say it...'

'Say what?' It was all going wrong. What was he talking about?

He lifted his head and met her eyes. 'Put simply,' he said, 'I've been thinking a good deal about the Albany Press. I've seen too many owner-managers fail because they were suspicious of enlisting help from outside, and I wouldn't like to see that happen to you. I've come up with a plan that I'm sure would benefit both of us.'

Her first impulse, quickly subdued, was to burst into wild, hysterical laughter. It was like walking down a final step that wasn't there and falling flat on your face. She felt her jaw drop, her eyes widen. Then from somewhere she found the words. 'I'm not sure,' she said in a voice she didn't recognise, 'that I know what you're talking about.'

He sat down beside her now, suddenly enthusiastic, completely unaware that he had just shocked her out of her mind. 'Well, this is my idea and it would need quite a bit of talking over, of course, but I'm sure that if you gave it serious consideration you'd agree that it has possibilities. As I told you, I'm very interested in printing and...'

Philippa had stopped listening. She dug her fingernails into her palms and bit into her bottom lip until she tasted blood. She would never have believed she could hurt so much. Nothing that Derek had ever said or done had sent pain ripping through her like this. She had believed Bart was falling in love with her and instead he'd been scheming to take over her printing presses.

Struggling for composure, she held up a hand. 'Just a minute.'

Something in her tone stopped Bart's eager flow of words. Something in her expression must have warned him he was on losing ground.

'No?' He looked almost comically disappointed.

'Definitely no.' It was easy to sound cold when ice was splintering in your veins. 'I'd hoped you understood that I won't tolerate any interference. I just want to be left alone to manage my business in my own way.'

It would have been better to leave it there but she found herself running on, almost out of control. 'You've been softening me up, haven't you? Manipulating me? What did Robert tell you about me? That I'm a poor, weak female? Is this the way you operate if the client is a woman? Ask them out, worm your way into their friendship? Well, I can tell you . . .' Her voice stuck humiliatingly in her throat.

'Aren't you over-reacting a little, Philippa?' Bart said, and there was a hard note in his voice. 'It was merely a suggestion, and you didn't even listen to what I had to say. And as for softening you up—rubbish! I asked you out because I wanted to, nothing to do with my offer or your brother. You're confusing two quite separate things.'

'Am I indeed?'

'Yes, damn it, you are,' he shouted.

It was the first time she'd heard anger in his voice and her inside quivered just as it had used to do when Father had vented his wrath on her.

For a moment they glared at each other, and then he went on more quietly, 'If that's what you believe I suppose I can't stop you. The truth is I *wanted* to take you out, to get to know you better because you're a very attractive young woman. It was a perfectly natural thing to do—it didn't have strings attached.'

Philippa turned her head away in silence, her bottom lip quivering ominously. She bit it hard.

Bart leaned towards her and his tone was his usual, reasonable one as he said, 'Won't you at least consider my suggestion?' He covered her cold hand with his. 'Believe me, Philippa, you're not going to keep going unless you do modernise your printing shop.'

'That's your opinion,' she said stiffly. 'I haven't asked for it.'

She drew her hand away and stood up. 'I'm rather tired. Perhaps you'd go now.'

He got to his feet, looking down into her small, flushed face. He said, oddly serious, 'The business is very important to you, isn't it, Philippa?'

She threw back her head defiantly. 'It's the most important thing in the world to me.' At that moment she could almost believe it was true.

'I see.' He nodded slowly, thoughtfully, as though he'd just come to understand and accept the situation. 'Oh, well, forget the whole thing. I shouldn't have brought it up at the end of a delightful evening. If you should change your mind...'

'I shan't change my mind.' She set her mouth into a stubborn line.

'Nevertheless...' He hesitated for a moment, then took out his wallet and extracted a business card. Philippa took the card, resisting an insane urge to tear it up and fling it in his face.

He smiled at her. Bart was himself again, she
thought bitterly—charming, too charming by half. He
said briskly, 'Well, I'll be getting along, then. Don't
come down all that way; I'll let myself out and close
the front door behind me.'

Portly strolled towards her from the doorway at that
moment and she stooped to pick him up, laying her
cheek against his soft fur, willing herself not to give
way until Bart had gone.

Bart looked down on the dark glossy head bent over
the cat. She was so small and vulnerable and gallant,
wrestling with a task that was doomed to failure, living
alone in this great barn of a house. He wanted to help
her, but she didn't want to be helped.

He badly wanted other things too, he thought wryly.
His eyes travelled down the soft swell of her breast,
the delicious curves of her as she stood fondling the
cat. She had felt so slight, so delicate in his arms. He
could almost have broken her with his two hands. He
had a strong urge to put his arms round her now, to
plead with her to let him help her, look after everything for her.

He took a step towards her and stopped. Better not,
caution advised. And anyway, she wouldn't be likely
to succumb to his fatal charm and fall into his arms.
Much safer to leave things as they were.

She raised her head a fraction but didn't meet his
eyes. 'Goodbye, Bart, and thank you for the theatre.
I enjoyed it very much.' Her voice was as wooden as
if she'd been a little girl saying her duty-thanks after
a child's party.

'Goodnight, Philippa,' he said and made his way
downstairs and out to his car.

*   *   *

Philippa wept for a long time after she heard the front door slam below, huddled in a corner of the sofa, with Portly curled up on her knees, purring loudly and quite oblivious to the emotional turmoil that was racking his mistress's small body.

She'd built Bart up into such a wonderful man, strong, sensitive, understanding, altogether admirable. He was totally different from Derek, from Father. He was falling in love with her, just as she was falling in love with him. He wasn't out to manipulate her; he was really interested in her for herself. And he had turned out to be just another self-centred man who was planning cynically to use her for his own ends. Probably, when he'd got the business advantage he wanted, he would have tried to entice her into his bed. That seemed to make it worse. Gulps of hysterical laughter mingled with her tears.

At last, exhausted, she dragged herself to the bedroom and pulled off her clothes. The violet jersey dress and the shawl lay in a heap on the floor and Portly, after an interested inspection, finally made himself comfortable in the middle of the heap. Philippa didn't care. She didn't think she'd ever wear them again.

She lay, shivering with cold and misery, listening to the wind howling round the tall old house. She hated him, she told herself, in bitter humiliation. *Hated* him!

That kiss up in the attic—the thing that had started all this nonsense in her own mind—had been merely the result of proximity. His dinner invitation, the looks he had given her from those brilliant dark blue eyes, had been calculated to charm, as had the present of the shawl he'd brought her. The visit to the theatre was to be the clincher, of course. Oh, yes, he'd been weighing up when the time was ripe to spring his proposition. His *business* proposition.

He'd behaved exactly as she might have expected if she'd known more about the business world she'd chosen to enter. He'd wanted something from her—a business deal—and he'd employed the usual method of trying to get it.

They called it corporate hospitality, didn't they? You selected your target and then sweetened him or her up. Wining and dining, invitations to the opera, to Wimbledon, to Lord's. It hadn't been quite as up-market as that in her case, but the method was the same. She blamed herself with a sick disgust for mixing business with—with what? Physical attraction. Lust, to put it brutally. Not love—of *course* not love.

She'd learned *nothing* from her experience with Derek, she thought savagely, tossing over in bed and dislodging the duvet to let in a stream of cold night air. Cursing, she pulled the duvet back.

There was only one point in her favour, she decided—at least she'd hung on to her pride. He couldn't have known what she'd been expecting, could he? Not that that mattered. She had absolutely no intention of ever seeing him again.

It was a warning, she told herself. No more pathetic adolescent fantasies! From now on she was going to put everything she had into her job. Modern girls didn't moon over men who didn't want them. If it happened to Chloe she would snap her fingers and dismiss him from her mind. But it would never happen to Chloe—she would never have been so feeble as to build a thrilling affair out of nothing at all. She would have known the score.

But at least she'd got things straight in her mind now. They called it adjustment to reality, didn't they? Tomorrow she would throw everything she had into the task of running the business, and forget all about Bart Marchant.

That resolve stimulated action. Philippa got out of bed, padded to the kitchen, filled the kettle and heated water for a hot-water bottle. She wrapped herself in a woolly cardigan before she crawled back into bed, curling up like Portly. Then both she and her cat were soon fast asleep.

Philippa spent the weekend spring-cleaning the office, then the flat. She wished she could spring-clean her mind, which kept presenting her with pictures and thoughts that no amount of hard physical work quite managed to blot out. But at least she tired out her body and fell into bed exhausted each night.

The following week she worked a ten-hour day. When she wasn't trying to get the accounts in order and write tactful letters to several creditors who were getting particularly pressing she was personally visiting all the customers on the firm's books, introducing herself as the new head of the Albany Press, and trying to establish herself as a forward-looking executive who would deal with their orders to their entire satisfaction.

A car would have probably made a better impression, but she didn't have a car. Father had got rid of his Rover when the business had smashed and had never bought another. She had learned to drive when she was engaged to Derek but he had never let her drive his speedy Volvo, and she had never wanted to.

So she walked, struggling with her umbrella in the
wind and the rain. The results of her treks were not
at all what she had hoped for. The managers she contacted—without exception male—regarded her with
an appreciative gleam in their eyes which had nothing
to do with any orders they might think of giving her.
Most were affable, one or two rather more than affable, but when she mentioned possible orders the
climate changed. Things were a little slow at
present...of course they would keep her in mind...but
just now... They shook their heads regretfully and
shook her hand rather more enthusiastically.

Thursday was crunch day. Even before Philippa
could open the morning post Ernie's bristly reddish
head appeared round the office door. 'Could I have
a word, Philippa?' His forehead was furrowed, and
his brown eyes met hers with an apologetic look as
he took the chair she indicated. He laced his fingers
together on his corduroy trousers and went straight
into the speech he had obviously been preparing.

'I feel very bad about this, luv,' he said. 'But it's
only fair to tell you.'

Philippa had a sinking feeling inside. She thought
she knew what was coming. 'Tell me what, Ernie?'
she helped him.

He shuffled his feet on the worn carpet. 'Well—the
fact is, we're rathered bothered, Ted and me. Young
Wayne doesn't figure in this—he'll be OK to get
another job, with the training he's had here already.'

'What are you saying, Ernie? You're not—not
giving notice, are you?'

Ernie looked horrified. 'Notice? Oh, no, luv, certainly not. It's just that—well, we'd like to know how
things stand. We can't help noticing that orders have

been very slack for some time and—and, what with some small firms around here going under...' He stopped, his brown eyes pleading with her to understand.

'You're wondering whether we are going to be able to carry on, is that it, Ernie? Whether your jobs are at risk?'

'That's it, luv. That's it exactly. You see, Ted's getting on now. He's not likely to get another job. And his missus is very poorly.'

'Oh,' Philippa said, quickly concerned. 'I didn't know.'

He nodded heavily. 'The doctors haven't said, but it seems likely she'll have to go in for an operation very soon. As for me—well, it doesn't seem important when you compare it, but the wife's got her heart set on booking this holiday in Spain. We've always planned to go abroad some day, when the children left home, and now we've finished paying for our Dawn's wedding we thought we'd book for Spain this summer. But of course it wouldn't do to book if...' He left the sentence hanging in the air.

Philippa nodded unhappily. She felt very cold. 'I'm afraid it's true, Ernie. Things aren't so good.' Then she brightened. 'But don't they say it's always darkest before the dawn? The annual order for Kenton's brochures will be coming along any day now, and that will keep us going for a good while, won't it? Look, leave it with me, will you? I'll go into the firm's situation very carefully and I'll let you know soon what's happening. Perhaps we could have a meeting, all of us, and talk things over?'

Ernie left, thanking her with his usual politeness but not, she thought, reassured.

Worse was to come. The morning post brought a letter from Kenton's, the firm's oldest and most valued customer. It wasn't even a personal letter from the chairman, John Kenton, an elderly man whom Philippa had met several times, but a printed letter stating that on the retirement of Mr John Kenton the company was inaugurating a complete refurbishment and updating and the office would be closed for the next three weeks.

That was bad enough, but what made it worse was that the circular letter had a coloured logo and was beautifully printed on top-quality paper, *but it hadn't been printed by the Albany Press*. After all these years Kenton's had taken their custom elsewhere.

Without even notifying her! She tossed the printed page into the waste-basket, trying to push down her disgust and disappointment. She'd been counting on the Kenton's order. She'd been so sure that she hadn't even been to visit them.

She was certainly not getting an easy introduction to her chosen career. Trying not to feel utterly deflated, Philippa got out her calculator and bank statements. If she could manage to get the money owed by Forrester's, the wine-bar people, there would be enough to pay the wages up to the end of next week. After that . . .

She spent the rest of the morning on the phone, trying to track down the manager of Forrester's without success. And by lunchtime she had to face the bitter truth: without a substantial injection of cash the Albany Press was finished. Her wonderful career as a company manager was over before it had begun.

She bit her lip hard to force back the tears. Managers didn't weep when things went wrong. A manager's job was to make decisions, Father had always told her. But he'd never let her take any responsibility. And now the biggest decision of all confronted her—the decision to admit failure.

Was it her fault—had there been anything she could have done to avert this? The answer was no. She took a long, hard look at the situation. What she owned was a very small printing company, with out-of-date equipment, working in the basement of a great barn of a house, which needed hundreds—no, thousands of pounds spending on repairs. And a sizeable overdraft, secured by the house. She wouldn't even have anywhere to live.

Philippa pushed her hair wearily back off her face. She supposed the wonder was that they'd been able to carry on so long. It was probably only because Ernie was such a star—he knew the printing business from top to bottom. She wondered why he had stayed on and guessed that it was out of loyalty to her. And now he'd be out of work—and poor Ted too. That was the worst thing of all, really. That was when she accepted the unpalatable fact that she would have to go to see Robert and eat humble pie and ask for his help. Robert would be cock-a-hoop. She could just see him smiling indulgently and taking everything over. Well, she might as well fix it up now. She'd see Robert tomorrow—make an appointment with him at his office.

Groaning inwardly, Philippa reached for the telephone.

CHAPTER SIX

ROBERT'S office was in one of the huge new office-blocks near Snow Hill Station in Birmingham. Philippa had never visited him here since he had moved in, a year ago. Next morning, as she pushed open the heavy swing door and crossed the spacious entrance hall to where a uniformed commissionaire sat behind a desk, she thought that Robert must be doing very well to have an office in this impressive building. Perhaps if she was very tactful and swallowed her pride he would help the Albany Press financially for a few months until she could get it on its feet again? She would try very hard.

The commissionaire looked up from his copy of the *Sun* to regard the pretty girl in the red coat with interest. 'Robert Price and Company? Fourth floor, miss. Lifts over there—can you manage?'

'Yes, thank you.' Philippa drew herself up to her full five feet four inches. Did she really look too small and insignificant to work a lift by herself, or did she just feel it? She summoned a lift and was sucked silently upwards at the touch of a button.

Even more luxury up here. A carpeted lobby with several doors and an enormous rubber plant in a copper urn. No wonder Robert considered the Albany Press insignificant! Compared with this prestige set-up, it was practically invisible, Philippa thought rather sadly.

The first door on the left, marked 'Robert Price and Company, Financial Services', led into an open-plan office. A young girl with cropped fair hair looked up from one of the three work-stations. 'Can I help you?'

The two other girls sitting in front of their computer screens were looking at Philippa with interest. They were pretty and well-groomed with shining hair and immaculate blouses. The whole place breathed efficiency, prosperity. Philippa felt out of place here in her unfashionable red coat.

'Philippa Price,' she said. 'Will you tell my brother I'm here?'

The receptionist gave her a friendly smile. 'Certainly, Miss Price. Do sit down.' She waved towards a chair and pressed a button on her desk.

Robert's office, when she was ushered into it, presented the same spacious atmosphere of prosperity as the rest of the building. Robert, immaculate as ever in pin-striped suit and white shirt, came across a swath of thick blue carpet to greet her.

He kissed her cheek, which surprised her. Robert wasn't much given to kissing. 'Well met, little sister, how are you?' he enquired jovially, leading her to a deeply upholstered visitors' sofa.

'I'm very well, Robert. How are you—and the family?'

'Thriving and growing apace.' He settled himself down beside her on the sofa. Very matey today, Philippa thought; she must take advantage of this unusually benign mood.

'Robert, I'm sure you're busy, so I'll come straight to the point. You see——'

There was a tap on the door and the receptionist came in with coffee on a tray.

'Thanks, Nicola, just put it down here.' Robert pulled a low table nearer to the sofa. 'You be mother,' he smiled at Philippa when the girl had gone.

Philippa poured coffee for them both from the blue pottery jug and added sugar for Robert.

'Thanks, dear. This is cosy, isn't it? An excuse to relax for a few minutes.' He drank his coffee and leaned back. 'I'm glad you called in, Pippa. I was going to ring you today anyway to fix up a meeting.'

'Oh, yes?' Philippa said cautiously. Robert was up to something—but what?

'Um, you see I've got some rather important news for you.' He cleared his throat and she realised that he was nervous.

'News?' she helped him.

'You may not be very pleased,' he went on, looking her straight in the eye, 'but I'm sure that when you think it over carefully you'll see that everything has worked out well.' He coughed again. 'Extremely well.'

Philippa put down her coffee-cup and leaned forward. 'Robert, what is all this? Do come to the point.'

'Yes. Well the point is that there's been rather a mix-up about Father's will. I saw Mr Bean yesterday—he's been off with flu for the last ten days—and it seems that Father made another will, later than the one I have here. Shortly before he was taken ill.' He paused.

Philippa was beginning to feel very cold. 'And?' she urged.

'And he must have thought better of burdening you with the house and the printing company. I expect he realised that the company was going downhill, and he must have wanted to take some of the responsibility from your shoulders.'

No, Philippa thought. No, no, *no*. But she sat very stiff, saying nothing.

'To put it in a nutshell,' Robert continued, taking another gulp of coffee, 'he left a small legacy to Chloe, the house to you, and the printing company to be shared equally between us.'

'Between the three of us?' Philippa whispered. All the breath had left her body.

'Oh, no. Just between you and me. So, you see, he intended us to be partners.' He laughed, and Philippa wanted to hit him. She felt rather sick.

Robert looked at her a trifle apprehensively. 'I'm afraid you're rather disappointed, little girl, but I'm sure it will all turn out for the best in the end.'

Philippa stared at him, stunned. Robert would take charge and she would go back to being a secretary again. I won't do it. I won't, she vowed, biting her lip. I'll get another job. I'll go abroad to Chloe and find something. I'll...

Robert patted her hand. 'That's the bad news,' he smiled. 'Now for some good news. As you may imagine, I couldn't possibly spare any time to devote to the Albany Press. Or any capital.' He pulled a wry face, gesturing round the luxury office. 'I've got plenty on my plate here. I had to think what would be best to do, and I intended to agree with you to wind up the business and cut our losses.'

Philippa swallowed over the huge lump in her throat. She wouldn't go down without a fight. 'But you couldn't do that. You only own half of it.'

'Exactly. So I'm at liberty to sell my half. It's the greatest good luck that I've found a buyer already. Of course, there is a good deal to be gone into. We have to get probate, and the books of the company will have to be audited, but I'm sure the deal will go through. The potential buyer is very interested in printing and he's dead keen to have a share in the business.'

Philippa's eyes felt as if they were popping out. A horrible suspicion was taking root in her mind. Oh, no—fate couldn't deal her yet another blow. 'Who is it?' she croaked.

'You know him already,' Robert said happily. 'He tells me you hit it off very well.'

Oh, God, it was, it was.

Robert stood up and pressed the intercom button. 'Nicola, get on to Mr Marchant, will you, and tell him I'd be delighted if he'd come along here as soon as he can?'

'Mr Marchant has just arrived, sir,' the girl piped, and a few seconds later the door opened and Bart walked into the room, hand outstretched.

'Hello, Philippa,' said Bart.

She couldn't stand up. Her legs wouldn't hold her. She sank deeper into the corner of the sofa and felt that the two large men before her were menacing figures from a crime movie.

Bart sat down beside her. 'Robert has told you? It's been a shock,' he said practically. 'I know how you feel.'

Oh, no, you don't know how I feel, she wanted to yell at him. I feel—betrayed. But you wouldn't understand that. You made up your mind to get something and you didn't care how you did it. She glared balefully at him.

He smiled, gripping her arm and shaking it gently. 'Dear Philippa,' he soothed. 'But it really isn't as bad as all that. When we've gone into everything you'll see that we shall get on very well as partners.'

A buzzer sounded on Robert's desk. The secretary's high piping voice announced something and Robert shrugged. 'You see how it is?' he murmured apologetically.

'You're busy,' Bart said. 'Come on, Philippa, let's go.' The pressure on her arm increased, urging her up.

'Go? Where to?'

'I'm driving you home; I've got an appointment in Stratford, and I'll drop you off on the way.'

She felt trapped. A spark of revolt surfaced. 'I don't want to go home.'

Robert said, with a tolerant smile, 'What were you thinking of doing, Pippa?'

She improvised wildly. 'I've got some—some shopping to do.'

He raised his brows in comic dismay. 'At the January sales? You're not up to that. Is she, Bart?'

'Certainly not,' Bart said firmly. 'She looks very pale. This had been a difficult day for her.'

Philippa glowered at the two of them, bending over her solicitously. 'Stop talking about me as if I were a parcel to be delivered,' she snapped. But she got to her feet, holding on to the arm of the sofa. Anything was better than staying in Robert's plush, airless office.

'Goodbye, Robert,' she said coldly.

He put a hand on her shoulder. 'Don't take it so hard, little sister,' he said. 'You'll see, it's all for the best.'

You keep on saying that, and for you it is, she thought. For you it couldn't be better—getting rid of your half of the business and pocketing whatever Bart is paying you for it, and getting rid of the responsibility you seem to feel for me, all at a stroke. Clever Robert! No wonder you're looking like the cat with the cream!

Bart put a hand at her elbow and led her out through the general office to the lobby. 'I'll just get my coat and a few things,' he said. 'I hang out over there.' He nodded towards the door on the opposite side of the lobby. 'Come in and sit down for a minute or two.'

'I'd rather wait here,' she said. 'I don't feel at home in these palaces of high finance,' she added with a feeble attempt at sarcasm.

He glanced at her uncertainly. 'You're OK, Philippa? You won't run away?'

'I won't run away.' Where did she have to run to—and what difference did it make?

She waited beside the rubber plant. Her legs really did feel very peculiar, and she hoped Bart wouldn't be long. When he reappeared he looked into her white face and said, 'My dear girl—you really do look rotten.'

'Thanks very much,' she whispered with a last vestige of spirit, and her legs finally gave up the struggle. Her knees sagged and Bart's arms came round her, holding her up.

'Come on,' he said masterfully. 'A little first aid is indicated.'

'This is—so silly,' she whispered as she felt herself being guided across the lobby and through the opposite door. She wasn't thinking at all clearly. Her mind felt as woozy as her knees. But it was marvellous to feel Bart's arms holding her, the warmth of his body so close to hers. She'd never expected to feel that particular strange thrill again, to smell that particular healthy masculine smell that belonged only to him.

Then she was lying on a sofa in what must have been his private office. She hadn't been conscious of getting here. Bart was standing looking down at her, his brow creased. 'You gave me quite a scare. Here, have a sip of this.' He held a glass to her lips.

She took a gulp of whatever it was, coughed, and came back quickly to reality. 'I didn't really faint, did I? I never faint.'

'Probably low blood sugar,' he told her practically. 'When did you last eat?'

'I had some coffee with Robert.'

'And dinner last night?'

'I don't know,' she admitted. She had a vague recollection of opening a tin of beans and throwing most of them into the waste-bin. Deciding to admit failure to Robert had done nothing at all for her appetite.

'I thought so,' Bart said angrily. 'You stupid girl, don't you even know how to look after yourself?'

She tried to lift her chin but it was difficult, as her head was propped against the back of the sofa. 'Of course I do. And it's my business what I eat or don't eat.' She sat up groggily and tried to get on her feet.

'Sit down,' Bart roared, and she was so surprised that she obeyed.

He went across to a desk and touched a button. A red-haired girl in a slim black skirt and white blouse appeared. 'Louise, do you think you could rustle up some sandwiches—and coffee?'

The girl bestowed a fleeting glance of curiosity upon Philippa and one of adoration upon Bart. 'Of course, Bart, straight away,' she crooned.

When she had gone he pulled up a small chair to the sofa and said worriedly, 'I don't like to see you in this state. What's been going on?'

She felt she was drowning in the depths of the dark blue eyes that held her own. 'Nothing's been going on... and why should you bother...?'

'It seems that I have your welfare at heart,' he told her with a twisted grin. 'Perhaps I don't want to lose my new partner so soon. You're very good at sending me packing when it suits you, but evidently you're incapable of looking after yourself.'

She said nothing. She hadn't the strength to argue with him at this stage—that would no doubt come later.

'Now you sit and relax while I tidy things up,' Bart said. 'Then we'll get you home.'

She watched him through half-closed eyes as he busied himself at the desk, tapping the computer keyboard with two fingers, frowning at the result, tapping again. The desk lamp threw his strong profile into bold relief. He wasn't exactly handsome, Philippa mused, her eyes tracing the way his dark brown hair curved behind his ears, but it was a face you wouldn't forget. The dominant nose, the broad forehead, slightly fuller over the eyes, the enigmatic tilt of the mouth, the whole look of the man seemed to have penetrated her consciousness until every part of it was as familiar to her as her own reflection in the glass. How was she ever going to get him out of her system?

He stood up with a sigh of satisfaction as the door opened to admit the girl called Louise, bearing a tray with a coffee-pot, two mugs, a jug and a plate of sandwiches.

'Thanks, Lou, you're an angel; put it on the desk.' Bart turned his charming smile on the girl and Philippa looked away. She knew that smile only too well. It must be very useful to him.

He put the plate on Philippa's knee. 'Eat up, lass. Coffee—black, I think.' He held the mug to her lips as if she were an invalid.

'I hate black coffee.' She pulled a face, but when he didn't take the mug away she sipped the bitter liquid unwillingly. It was hot and aromatic and she had to admit that she did feel better almost immediately. The sandwiches, on the other hand, looked tempting— moist brown bread with pink ham protruding at the edges. 'A fair exchange,' she mumbled as she bit into one of them hungrily.

'What?'

'We seem fated to ply each other with sandwiches.'

He was silent, looking thoughtfully at her. Then he said slowly and deliberately, 'I think, Philippa, that we seem fated to team up in other ways too.'

'Because we're probably going to be partners in my business?' She would *not* allow herself to interpret that lazy look, that deep, meaningful inflexion in his voice, as anything more than that. It was no doubt a habit with him, all part of the professional charm.

'Perhaps,' he said. 'Now, eat up your sandwiches and then we'll get going.'

Back in Leamington, three-quarters of an hour later, Philippa opened the front door with her key and picked up the letters strewn on the mat. Bart made to go upstairs, but Philippa said, 'I'll attend to the post first.' She went into the office and sank into the big chair behind the desk.

He followed her and stood beside the desk, glancing at his watch. 'I won't stay any longer now,' he said.

Philippa almost snapped back that she hadn't asked him to, and then she remembered. This wasn't her own office any more. For all practical purposes this man owned half of it.

'Before I go there are just one or two things,' he went on. 'I know it seems early days for me to start throwing my weight about, but I get the impression that things here may be a trifle urgent on the money front. Was that what you were coming to see Robert about?'

'Clever at summing things up, aren't you?' she said rather bitterly. 'I was coming with a white flag in my handbag. Robert was right, of course; the business here has gone too far to be saved, except with an input of capital, which Robert wasn't willing to provide. And when he found he was half-owner of the company he would have considered it even more of a waste, I'm sure. He told you about my father's will, and what happened?'

Bart was standing close to her chair, and she wished he'd move further away. She didn't look up at him but she was sure he was taking in everything she said. She was beginning to know what made him tick, she thought, and she didn't much like what she was finding out. He was the kind of person who led you on to talk and then used the information in any way that suited him. She herself, on the contrary, liked the whole truth out there in the open—everything on the table plainly.

'Yes,' he said. 'I met him by chance this morning, going up in the lift, and we had a chat. When I found out what the position was, regarding a possible sale of his half of the printing business, I jumped at it.'

She shook her head. 'I don't see why. We're not exactly a good buy.'

He raised dark brows. 'If you'd listened to what I had to say that night after the theatre you'd know why. You never ought to refuse to hear a business proposition.'

But I didn't think it was a business proposition, did I?

'I hope you don't think you can lecture me, now you've grabbed half my business,' she snapped.

His lips compressed. 'Please don't adopt that tone with me, Philippa.'

'What tone?'

'You know darned well what I mean.' He pulled the visitor's chair round the desk and sat down, facing her. 'Now let's get this straight; we've got quite a job to tackle together and it's never going to work if you go on being tetchy and resentful.'

'I'm not——' she began hotly, but he ignored her and ploughed on.

'It's very clear that you don't like the idea of working with me, and I must have cards on the table if we're to go on. I know you wanted to run the company by yourself, but that was never a possibility as things are. I could see that at a glance right from the beginning. I think you realise it now. So why won't you accept help? I'm all for independence, but your attitude seems a bit over the top. Come on, now, tell me straight out why you feel so badly about it.'

She almost laughed. What would he say if she said 'I wanted you to fall in love with me, but you only wanted a business arrangement'? She looked into the keen blue eyes and then down at the desk. She said, 'I think I feel—cheated.' That was true, at any rate.

'I don't much like that word.'

'You asked me how I felt. Well, I'll tell you.' At least she could tell him half the truth. 'I've been dominated and manipulated and pushed around by men all of my grown-up life. For a few heady days I thought I was free at last to please myself, to prove that I could do something worthwhile alone, instead of taking orders. And then—this.'

There was a long silence. She could feel his eyes on her but she couldn't make herself look up to meet them. He said slowly, 'Yes, I think I see what the trouble is. The only thing I can suggest is that you believe me when I say that I've no intention of dominating you, and in spite of your dark suspicions——' he grimaced wryly '—I never had any intention of trying to manipulate you. If you can believe me, and agree to work amicably with me, I know we can save your company. If not, I pull out of the deal before we go any further. Which is it to be?'

He walked to the window and stood looking out, his hands in his pockets, his back to her. He was playing her like a fish on a hook, she knew. She didn't doubt that he meant what he said. If she refused to work with him he would take back his offer to buy Robert's share of the company, and the company would be wound up.

She stared at his tall, straight back and wished she could see his face. Did he care at all, personally, whether she agreed or not? Whether she would drift out of his life for good?

She pulled her thoughts back. There was Ted and his sick wife—and Ernie with his long-worked-for holiday in Spain—and Wayne, who had nearly finished his apprenticeship. And all the firms they owed money to, as well. She remembered vaguely what an awful time it had been when the family business had failed three years ago. This wouldn't be as traumatic as that perhaps, but still...

But most of all she knew that she couldn't make a choice that would mean she would never see Bart Marchant again. She might be laying up a load of misery for herself, but she couldn't help that.

He swivelled round suddenly. 'Well?'

'I can't see that I have any choice,' she said.

Bart's face cleared. 'Good,' he said, and held out a hand across the desk. 'Partners?'

'Partners,' agreed Philippa, taking his hand briefly, wishing—wishing—oh, never mind what she was wishing. He came and sat down in the chair behind the desk. 'Now, before I go, is there anything pressing at the moment?'

He had asked for it, and he was going to get it. 'Too true there is. These——' she pushed over a folder containing a sheaf of bills '—and there's just enough money in the kitty to pay wages for next week, and not much hope of getting any more in before then.'

He glanced through the stack of bills without blinking. He was probably used to dealing with companies who dealt in millions of pounds every day. 'No problem,' he said crisply. 'Just give me a note of your bank and the name of the account and I'll transfer some cash straight away.'

She wrote on a notepad and handed him the particulars.

'And if you've no objection it might be a good idea if I have a front-door key?'

She said rather wearily, 'Would it make any difference if I did object?'

'Certainly it would,' he said rather stiffly. 'I haven't yet any claim on you or the business. There may even yet be some hidden legal snag, I'm well aware of that. But, as a rescue operation, I'm willing to top up the kitty in advance.'

She nodded. 'Yes. I suppose I should be grateful, but at the moment I don't feel anything much. I'm glad the men aren't going to lose their jobs, though. And of course you can have the keys.' She opened a desk drawer and took out a duplicate set of keys. 'Front door, office, outside door to the printing shop; that's the lot.'

'Thanks,' he said, putting them in his pocket and making no comment on her lack of enthusiasm.

'Can I tell Ernie his job's safe?'

'Oh, I think we can risk that, don't you?' This was how it was going to be. He'd pretend to consult her, but really he would decide everything, supply the capital, give the orders.

He was watching her face closely. As if he'd read her thoughts, he said, quite gently. 'We make decisions together, Philippa?'

'Oh, yes? I was wondering where I fitted in.'

'You're going to do all the hard work, my girl. Until we get the new company established we'll be working together, consulting, talking things over. Then you'll be managing the show, not me. I'll just be a sleeping partner.' He eyed her laughingly. 'I should be so lucky, as they say.' He got to his feet. 'I'll come back later on and we can have a talk. That suit you?'

'Yes, I suppose so,' she said resignedly.

He leaned down and peered into her face. 'Don't look so enthusiastic.' He put a finger under her chin and tweaked it up. 'I'm not a difficult bloke, you know. You might even enjoy working with me.'

When he'd gone Philippa sat very still, the back of her hand on her chin where his finger had rested. Then, abruptly, she began to open the letters. Two bills, three advertisements, and a letter from Chloe. She opened it eagerly. Chloe seemed like a link with sanity after the extraordinary morning.

Darling Sis, no time for a long letter. Have been on a trip to Cannes with the boss—strictly business, I hasten to add. This is just to alert you that I'm sending you a present from Paris. It should arrive any time. It's rather big, but I'm sure you'll find it fun. Bye for now, sweet sis. Chloe.

Philippa smiled fondly. It was like Chloe, who had a pleasant habit of giving presents at odd moments. Something big? And fun? She could do with some fun, she thought. She folded up the letter and went down to interview Ernie.

Understandably the men were delighted to hear that the Albany Press was safe, and no negative note was sounded about Bart's involvement. 'Sounds like a good idea, luv,' Ernie said, 'you've had too much on your own shoulders. And Mr Marchant seems a good man—knows quite a bit about printing, too. He was very interested in those old presses.'

'We'll have to see about updating the presses,' she said. 'I'll let you know how things go.'

Ernie was looking up through the basement window. 'Someone up there, snooping,' he said.

He walked over to the window and took a closer look. 'It's a young gentleman. He's waving. Shall I go up and see what he wants?'

'I'll go,' Philippa said. 'Perhaps it's a customer. Someone who wants to give us a big exciting order.'

She went up the outside steps. A slim young man with intelligent dark eyes, sleek black hair flopping across his forehead, and wearing a light blue designer suit, stood beside the railings.

'Were you looking for me?' Philippa enquired.

The sloe-black eyes smiled hopefully into hers. 'Miss Price?'

'Yes.'

'Pascal Maurois. I come from your sister. She has written to you, yes?'

'From Chloe?' She had forgotten all about Chloe's letter. '...a present from Paris...I'm sure you'll find it fun.' Understanding dawned. How like Chloe, and what an inappropriate time for the arrival of a visitor! But Chloe hadn't known about this morning's happenings and the deep gloom they had cast over Philippa's world.

The young man's face had fallen. 'It is not a convenient time to call upon you?'

Philippa pulled her thoughts together and held out her hand. 'Yes, of course it is. Chloe's letter wasn't clear, that's why I was a bit confused. Do come in.'

He held her hand and leaned towards her as if he was going to kiss her on both cheeks, French-fashion, but then drew back.

Philippa led the way into the house. 'My flat is on the second floor,' she said over her shoulder. She couldn't very well ask him to come into the office.

He padded lightly up the stairs, and into the living-room after her. 'But what a charming *appartement*, so very correct for its charming owner.' The sloe-black eyes danced wickedly into hers. 'I am a designer, *vous savez*, and I know about beautiful décor—and beautiful women.'

I bet you do, Philippa thought, amused in spite of herself. 'Would you like a drink? Have you had lunch, Monsieur Maurois?'

'Oh, please, you must call me Pascal—and I have not lunched. I came, hoping you would do me the honour of taking you to lunch.' He must have seen a refusal hovering on Philippa's lips, for he added winningly, 'And then I shall tell you all about your sister and her news. You will come—please?'

'Well, thank you very much—Pascal.'

She would do as she liked, and if Bart came back and expected to find her here, meekly waiting for him to arrive for a discussion of ways to carve up her business to suit himself, then he would have to think again.

She smiled brilliantly at the young Frenchman. 'Do sit down,' she said. 'I won't keep you long.'

And as she went into her bedroom to attend to her hair and make-up she felt a distinct lifting of her spirits. There were other men in the world besides Bart Marchant.

CHAPTER SEVEN

'You will not object to what you call a "pub lunch",
I hope?' Pascal enquired as he handed Philippa into
a taxi ten minutes later. 'I have heard that they serve
a very good lunch at an 'otel beside the river.'

'I'd love a pub lunch,' she assured him. The ham
sandwiches in Birmingham seemed a long time ago,
and she wanted to forget the circumstances of that
little episode as quickly as possible.

It was one of those rare days that occasionally happened in January—mild and sunny. Pascal settled
Philippa at a table for two in the window of the busy
bar-room, full of chatter and the clink of plates and
glasses. 'I will go and find what they have to offer.
You like quiche?'

'Love it,' Philippa said. She watched him join the
crowd lining the bar and then turned to look out of
the window across the Pump Room Gardens towards
the river, and thought that this was quite the nicest
thing that had happened to her for ages.

'Now tell me all about Chloe,' she said when an
appetising-looking bacon and mushroom quiche had
been set before her.

Pascal's sloe-dark eyes danced with mischief as he
slid into the chair opposite. 'I tell you about myself
first, yes? You wish to know all about me?'

'Of course,' she said, mock-repentant. 'That is
much more important to me.'

He needed no further encouragement. He told her about his home in Provence, his parents, his two sisters, his ambition to become a famous designer. He had passed his exams, he announced proudly, and was working for an industrial-design partnership in Paris. He was in England, doing a short course at Warwick University, and was returning to Paris tomorrow.

'And now at last we arrive at how I know your sister Chloe. You like the wine?' He filled up her glass.

She smiled dreamily. She was beginning to feel slightly hazy. 'Lovely—it tastes of spring flowers.' Oh, lord, why did she have to think of spring flowers just when she was beginning to forget about Bart Marchant? 'Tell me how you know Chloe.'

Pascal was gazing lingeringly across the table at her. 'Chloe? Ah, yes. You see, there are family connections. *Mon oncle*, he is head of the firm for which I work. He is also the lover of your sister, Chloe.'

'I see,' Philippa said slowly, 'you are Claude's nephew? Claude—Maurois, is it? Chloe didn't mention his second name.'

'*Oui*. Claude is my father's brother. He is a very fine man. I admire him.'

'That's nice,' Philippa said rather lamely.

'And one other thing.' Pascal tapped his nose mysteriously. 'I am almost sure they will marry shortly.'

'*Really*?' Now that *was* interesting.

'Really, truly.' Pascal's dark eyes laughed into hers. 'And, if I guess right, you will come to Paris for the wedding, yes? I would be most honoured to escort you to see the—how would you say?'

'To see the sights? Oh, yes, I'd enjoy that very much.'

By the time lunch was over Pascal was no longer a stranger, he was almost a member of the family. They could have walked back to Albany Square, but he insisted on ringing for a taxi.

'I *have* enjoyed myself; thank you so much, Pascal,' Philippa said warmly as he helped her from the taxi, holding her hand much longer than was necessary.

'I too have enjoyed myself exceedingly. It is a pity I return to Paris tomorrow; I should have liked very much for us to meet again. I wished to see you sooner but this has been a very busy week for me.' He pulled a doleful face and then cheered up. 'I shall look forward to meeting you again in Paris when you visit your sister. *Au revoir*, Philippa.' He kissed her rather slowly on both cheeks, got back into the taxi and was driven away with a final wave.

Philippa waved back. It was only as she turned to mount the steps to the front door that she saw Bart standing at the office window. From this distance his face looked as black as thunder.

For a moment she was tempted to pretend she hadn't seen him, and go straight up to the flat, but that would look childish. She sauntered into the office, still feeling the confidence-boosting effect of the last couple of hours.

'Hello—you came back?' She sank gracefully into her big chair. 'Did you want something?'

Perhaps she'd been wrong about the black-as-thunder look. He seemed just as suave as ever now, leaning against the desk casually.

'I did say I'd come back to talk about things. You didn't say you were going out.'

'I didn't know. An old friend from Paris turned up unexpectedly. I do so hope you haven't been waiting long,' she added sweetly.

He gave her an exasperated look. 'At least *I've* been getting down to some work.' He indicated the books strewn over the desk.

'While I've been playing?'

'No criticism implied,' he said. 'Let's not waste time sparring, enjoyable though it may be.' He had evidently been sitting in Father's big chair, but now he pulled the visitor's chair round the desk and sat down, indicating that she do the same.

She continued to stand. 'If we're going to be partners we should start on an equal footing. I propose we get rid of this chair.' She looked at the big director's chair rather wistfully, thinking of the way she'd planned to sit here, the owner-manager of a thriving company. She'd certainly been indulging in some fantasies lately!

He grinned. 'Now you're getting the hang of it.' He removed both chairs to the far side of the office and placed two small upright chairs one each side of the desk.

Philippa sat down. 'That's better.' She smiled back. Perhaps it would be all right. Perhaps he wasn't going to throw his weight about. 'Tell me the worst,' she said.

For an hour he talked and she listened, and as she listened she was more and more conscious of his lightning grasp of everything connected with the situation of the company, and her own abysmal ignorance of management.

At last she shook her head. 'I didn't realise Father had lost his grip on things to that extent,' she said. 'I wish he'd confided in me.'

Bart sat back in his chair and regarded her puzzledly. 'You didn't know? Then what exactly *did* you do here, Philippa?'

'I kept the books, answered the telephone, typed the letters, sent out the bills, did the filing, and occasionally acted as peacemaker between the print shop and the office. Father wasn't too popular with the men.' She sighed. 'He wasn't an easy man.' She considered for a moment. 'I suppose I should have realised that orders were falling off, but even if I had, there wouldn't have been anything I could do about it. Father did all the dealing with customers himself and managed the finances. He never discussed anything like that with me.'

'Hm,' he mused, and the sound spoke volumes.

'Go on, say it out loud,' Philippa challenged.

'Say what?'

'What an ignorant, conceited creature I am, to imagine I could tackle all this mess——' she gestured at the littered desk '—on my own. I wanted——' She broke off, biting her lip, the tears not far away.

He smiled at her, his devastating smile. 'I know what *I* want,' he said. 'I want three cups of tea. Will you invite me up to your eyrie and do the needful?'

'Oh, yes, *what* a good idea.' The grey eyes glistened with unshed tears through her answering smile as she got to her feet. 'Come along up.' She stopped. 'What's wrong?' He hadn't moved and he was looking at her fixedly.

'Nothing's wrong. I was just thinking that your eyes are like stars.'

The shock made her blink. For a breathless moment she searched his face. A few days ago she would no doubt have imagined there was an enquiry in his. Now she knew he was merely fooling, perhaps delivering a small compliment because he felt sorry for her. But she didn't want his pity for her inadequacy as a businesswoman. She laughed merrily. 'How poetic! Now you own half a printing press you'll be able to print your first slim volume of poems all by yourself—won't that be nice?' She didn't wait for his response but raced away upstairs and into her kitchen.

He followed and stood watching in silence as the kettle boiled and she popped two tea-bags in the pot and filled it up. She put the remainder of a banana and coconut cake on a plate. 'Sugar?'

'Hm?' he said vaguely. 'Oh—no sugar, thanks. Just milk.'

He trailed after her as she carried the tray to the low table by the fire. He sat down on the sofa and stared into the bars of the fire for what seemed a very long time. Philippa glanced at him as she filled his cup and pushed it towards him. She was trying to think of something to say when he suddenly gave her a beaming smile and burst out, 'Philippa, you're a marvel.'

She had to keep up the joke, though she had no idea what it was all about. 'Oh, yes, I know that. But why, especially?'

'You've come up with the most brilliant idea I've heard for a long time. What you said down in the office about printing my own slim volume of poems—that's it.'

'Oh, yes?' she encouraged politely. This kind of easy banter between the sexes was new to her. Derek hadn't indulged in anything so light-hearted. But she seemed to slip into it quite naturally.

However, it seemed that he wasn't joking. He accepted a large slice of cake absently and went on, 'You see, all I've been thinking about is the financial angle, but you've put your finger on something just as important in its own way. Specialisation.'

'Go on,' Philippa said, watching him. His whole face was lit up by enthusiasm. He looked absolutely fabulous. I can't help loving him, she thought helplessly. What am I going to do?

He gulped down a second cup of tea and proceeded to explain. 'I have a smallish interest in a publishing firm in Birmingham. They publish small books with a nature slant—plants and animals, that kind of thing. And also some children's books.' He paused, surveying the ceiling. 'Now I wonder! Strike while the iron is hot. I'll go down and give John Pargeter a ring straight away.' He raised one thumb and strode out of the room.

Well! thought Philippa indignantly. The great manipulator in action! Consultation? Planning together? That was a joke. The moment a new scheme occurred to him he was rushing off to put it into action. If she wanted to keep her head above water, let alone keep a vestige of her independence, she was going to have to fight.

She collected the tea things and went into the kitchen to wash them up. She was doing her best to fuel her wrath into a good old blaze when she heard Bart's steps running back up the stairs and her knees felt weak.

He came storming into the kitchen. 'Great news! I got John himself and put the idea to him as a possibility—that we should take over the printing of their children's books. That would be a splendid start for us when we get the new colour presses installed. Ernie will take the printing in his stride, I'm sure. I'd like to set up a design studio and photographic room too, if funds will run to it. It would be more fun to do the whole job ourselves. We could cost it out and . . .' He stopped.

Philippa was standing at the sink, her back to him. He put his hands on her shoulders and turned her round. 'You're pleased with the idea?'

She said, 'It seems a bit late to ask me that now. You've arranged it all.' She kept her eyes fixed on the top button of his jacket.

He looked crestfallen. 'Oh, Philippa, I'm sorry. I got rather carried away—I don't usually. You'll have to remind me when I'm overstepping the mark.'

He was so reasonable. So plausible. Suddenly she wanted to believe him, to trust in him utterly. She raised limpid grey eyes to his and a tiny smile touched the corners of her mouth.

His hands were still on her shoulders. She could feel the warmth of them through the fine wool of the oyster-coloured jumper she had worn to go out to lunch with Pascal.

Their eyes locked and she couldn't look away. The moment stretched and stretched. She felt she was drowning in a deep blue sea. His face came closer and he said softly, 'I'm afraid I can't resist you, you bewitching child.'

Resistance didn't occur to her either. When his mouth touched hers her whole body went warm and languid. Her eyelids drooped and she yearned towards him, locking her hands in the crisp hair at the back of his head, letting her lips relax, her tongue curl to his.

The kiss went on and on and she felt herself arch towards him in an uncontrollable spasm of excitement. His mouth lowered to nuzzle into her neck, and when one hand closed over her breast she let out a little cry at the sharp, delicious sensation that spiralled down her body. This was heaven—this was what she'd never known in all her life. She wanted more of it—more. She wanted to know everything, to experience everything——

Somewhere downstairs the front doorbell jangled. Stopped. Jangled again. With a tremendous effort Philippa pulled slightly away, her hands going to her hair. 'I must go down,' she croaked.

'Leave it,' Bart said impatiently.

'No, it might be important.'

'Oh, lord—*this* is important,' he groaned. His face was contorted with longing; he looked desperate.

Suddenly Philippa felt a strange sense of surprise. She had this power over him. She wasn't merely a helpless pawn in his game of business after all.

Quite calmly she said, 'We can't afford to let any opportunity slip, can we? I'd better go down and see who it is.'

She went down and opened the front door, only to find that whoever had rung the bell had gone. Even more slowly she climbed up to the flat again.

Bart was slumped on the sofa in the living-room. He stood up when she came in and held out a hand to her. 'Let's go on where we left off,' he said. His smile wasn't quite as confident as usual.

'I don't think so.' She ignored his hand.

He came closer and reached for her, but she moved away. 'Why not?' he said, puzzled.

On the journey downstairs and upstairs again Philippa had had time to gather her wits together. 'There really isn't any reason now, is there? You've got what you wanted.' Where did that cool little voice come from?

'What I——? Oh, *that* old thing! You don't really believe I'd be such a swine as to make up to you for what I could get out of it, do you?'

She bit her lip. 'I...don't know. Men—do that sort of thing.' Too true, she thought, remembering Derek.

'Well, I don't.' He took her by the shoulders and shook her angrily. 'And I *haven't* got what I want. I want to take you into the bedroom and undress you and make love to you. I've wanted that ever since I came here that first day, when you practically threw me out. It's just that I've tried not to rush you.'

She shook her head. 'No,' she said again.

His arms were round her now, drawing her closer. 'You want to, don't you? You want it as much as I do. Then why not?' he pleaded. 'We're going to be together, to work together. Let's live together too. I'd make it good for you. I'd look after you. I shan't marry again—you know that—but I'd be faithful to you, I promise.'

Her face was pressed against his shirt. She could feel his heart throbbing heavily. She made an attempt to shake her head. 'No,' she whispered again.

He still held her. 'Oh, Philippa,' he groaned desperately, 'you don't know what it's like.'

It was the hardest thing she'd ever done in her life not to give in but somehow she must do it. An affair was what he was offering—what she had at one time been all poised to accept. But that was in another life, before she had fallen in love with him, when she had seen herself as a modern career-woman like Chloe, taking affairs in her stride. But it was too late now, she thought sadly. She wanted much more than an affair; she wanted his love, and he hadn't even hinted that he loved her.

She drew away and it was like wrenching herself in half. 'I'm sorry, Bart,' she said, 'but it wouldn't do, and if you think about it you'll agree. One shouldn't mix business with—with an affair. It wouldn't work.'

She held her breath until her throat felt like bursting. *Please* say it isn't an affair you want. Say you love me and want us to commit ourselves to each other. Forsaking all others. Oh, you don't have to marry me, it would be enough to love and cherish...if you love me...

But he didn't say it. He stood looking down at her and his face was granite-hard. 'So it was true what you told me. Your business *is* the most important thing in your life.'

'I don't remember...' she faltered.

He wasn't listening. He walked to the window and stood looking down. The noise of the traffic rumbled in the distance and the wind gusted through the trees in the square. At last Bart turned abruptly and said, 'You're probably right, it wouldn't do. So from now on it's strictly business between us. That's how you want it?' He didn't sound angry any longer, but there was no friendliness, no warmth in his voice.

She nodded. She couldn't speak that enormous lie aloud.

'Right,' he said. 'Well, then, suppose we discuss *together* my idea of going into book printing? The sooner we begin to transform the business, the better. What do you think?' He glanced at his watch. 'We could slip out for a quick meal a bit later, and have the whole evening before us.'

I couldn't, Philippa thought desperately. Not now, this minute. Tomorrow, perhaps. 'I'm sorry,' she said. 'I'm afraid I can't. I have a dinner-date.' The lie slipped out automatically.

He gave her a nasty look. 'With your Parisian friend, of course! So there *is* something more important than your business, after all.'

She stared back. 'Don't be childish, Bart.'

They were like two cats, Philippa thought, growling at each other, sizing each other up. One of them would have to retreat in the end but it wasn't going to be her.

Bart shrugged. 'We're not going to get anywhere today, I can see that. I'll call in tomorrow afternoon on my way home, and hope to find you in a better frame of mind.'

'Very well,' she said stiffly. She thought, Just *go* before I finally lose my cool and start to scream.

'I left my coat down in the office,' he said. 'I'll pick it up on the way out. Goodnight, Philippa.'

'Goodnight, Bart,' she said politely and watched him walk out of the room.

A moment or two later the front door closed with a muted slam. Philippa sat down rather quickly. What had she done? She must be mad to send him away. Perhaps if they'd had an affair he would, in time, have found he loved her. Perhaps...

But it was much more likely that he would have tired of her inexperience very quickly. 'A soppy little virgin,' Derek had called her. She had no real experience of how to please a man, certainly not an urbane, sophisticated man like Bart. At least, she consoled herself, one of her resolutions was still intact. She was her own mistress, although she had declined to be his. She had just made a decision and she would stick by it, however much it hurt. Not, she thought bleakly, that he was likely to ask her again. Her heart shook as she remembered that hard, angry look on his face. He wasn't a man who would take kindly to being rejected.

She wondered what had happened to break up his marriage. He had sounded so desolate when he had spoken of Paula; he must have loved her very much—perhaps still did. Ah, well, she'd never know what had happened, he'd never tell her. The boundary line had been drawn; they were business partners now and that was all.

A soft brush against her legs announced the arrival of Portly, and Philippa leaned down and gathered him into her arms. '*You* love me, don't you, my cat?' she sighed, and he placed a velvet paw delicately against her cheek as if in reply. The big house felt a little less lonely as she hugged him. 'Let's go and find you some dinner.'

She went into the kitchen, fed Portly, and made a beef-paste sandwich and a cup of coffee for herself. Before she could eat it the phone rang down in the office. Bart? she thought. Perhaps to tell her he was sorry for the way they had parted? She raced down the stairs. First thing tomorrow she must get an extension phone put up in the flat, she promised herself as her heel caught in the worn carpet and she lurched forward, grabbing the rail.

Her palms were damp as she lifted the receiver. Chloe's voice came to her over the wire. 'Hello, little sister, how are you?'

Philippa sank weakly into a chair. 'Oh, I'm fine—fine. Lovely to hear you,' she croaked.

'You don't sound very fine. Are you OK—really?'

'Yes—really. A bit thrown off balance, that's all. Things have been happening today.'

'What things?' Chloe asked quickly.

'Haven't you heard from Robert?'

'No, not a chirp.'

'I thought he might have rung you,' Philippa said, trying to gather her wits together. 'Well, he sprung it on me this morning. Father left another, later, will and it's quite different.'

She heard Chloe's gasp and hurried on, 'You get a small legacy.'

'Really? That was big of him. I imagined he'd cut me out.'

'He evidently had second thoughts about everything. One of them was that he didn't leave the house and the business to me, as we understood at first. The printing business—which I was so banking on being my own—isn't. He left it equally divided between Robert and me.'

'Oh, my poor sweet,' Chloe groaned. 'So you're going to have Big Brother breathing down your neck after all.'

'Well, not exactly,' Philippa went on rather awkwardly. 'Robert has lost no time in selling off his half of the business. So Robert isn't going to share the business with me. It's a man called ...' she swallowed '...Bartholomew Marchant.'

She heard Chloe's chuckle and thought, Yes, that's how I felt before I met him. She went on hastily, 'He's a management consultant in quite a big way.'

'Oh,' Chloe said. 'I don't like management consultants much. What's this individual like?'

Philippa searched wildly in her mind for words to describe Bart. 'Oh—thirtyish, dark and forceful—what you'd expect.'

'Oh, dear, I *am* sorry, he sounds a real bastard,' Chloe commiserated. 'I know the type. He'll be worse than Father at bossing you around; the younger ones always think they're little tin gods.'

'No, you're wrong, Chloe,' Philippa said hastily. 'Bart isn't like that at all.'

There was a silence. '*Bart*?' Chloe queried gently.

'Well, I couldn't very well call him Bartholomew, could I?'

Another silence. Then Chloe said, 'He's OK, is he? I think I'd better come over and see what's going on.'

Philippa managed a laugh. 'Nothing's going on—that is, nothing I can't cope with. I'm getting quite educated in the ins and outs of business.'

'I wasn't thinking of business,' Chloe said drily. 'Well, this is the most extraordinary news. I suppose I must possess my soul in patience until I hear more from you. By the way, how did you get on with Pascal? Has he contacted you yet?'

'Oh, yes,' Philippa told her brightly, relieved to change the subject. 'We had lunch together today. He's a nice boy.'

'Good work. Are you seeing him again?'

'No, he's going back to Paris tomorrow. And Chloe—I don't want to pry, but——'

'I know what you're going to say,' Chloe broke in. 'I suppose Pascal has guessed that Claude and I—his uncle and I—have decided to get married.' She chuckled. 'I'm afraid it's true. I never thought I was going to give in, but Claude's very persuasive and I came round to it in the end. And after lecturing you about how satisfactory affairs are too!' Her voice dropped a tone. 'Trouble is, I'm in love with the man.'

'Oh, Sis, it's marvellous news,' Philippa said warmly. It was lovely to be able to be unconditionally glad about something. 'I hope you'll be very, very happy.'

'I think we will. We're both fairly mature people.'

'Will you give up your job?'

'Oh, no, Claude wouldn't hear of it. He knows how much it means to me. You'll come over for the wedding?'

'Try to stop me. When's it going to be?'

'Within the next couple of months, probably, as soon as we can both manage the time off for a short honeymoon. Try to come over a few days before— I'm longing for you to meet Claude.'

Philippa promised she would, and chatted on happily for a while longer. When she put the phone down her eyes were wet. Darling Chloe, she'd sounded so—different, somehow. Softer, more serene. That was what happened when you knew that the man you loved loved you, Philippa supposed. She wondered bleakly if she would ever know that bliss herself.

At the moment it didn't seem at all likely.

CHAPTER EIGHT

IN THE weeks that followed Philippa realised the truth of the saying that a man was able to live his life in separate compartments—which usually meant dividing his job from his love-life. She guessed that Bart, with his disciplined mind, could do that quite easily. He had almost certainly put her into a compartment labelled 'For business only', and that was how he treated her.

He was unfailingly courteous, tactful, even occasionally jokey, and he went out of his way to involve her in every detail of the complicated transfer. But never did he give a hint that he remembered the moments when he had held her in his arms and told her he wanted desperately to make love to her. Sometimes, looking at his intelligent, rather stern face, she wondered if it had ever happened.

But she knew it *had* happened, and if he could erase it from his mind like drawing a brushful of correction fluid over a line of type then she couldn't. She was in love and, no matter how hard she tried to concentrate on business matters, the very fact of Bart's presence—or absence—coloured every moment of every day.

They were constantly in each other's company. Transferring Robert's share of the business and setting up a partnership between herself and Bart involved endless meetings—with solicitors, accountants, auditors, bank managers.

There were long discussions with Ernie about the updating of the presses in the printing shop, and, although Philippa hesitated to join them, pleading that she knew nothing about the technical side of the printing business, Bart insisted on her being present. 'A manager should know everything that goes on in her business,' he insisted. 'And don't you dare take that as a criticism, Philippa. I'm well aware that you've had no opportunity to learn.' He smiled at her suddenly, the smile that made her weak at the knees, and added, 'At a pinch I'll teach you myself.'

Philippa had to admit the truth of what he said and did her best to pick up something of the basics of the printing process as the two men jabbered away about the merits and demerits of different colour printers, folding-and-trimming machines, computer typesetting and camera equipment—all the myriad details that seemed to comprise a modern design and printing firm. It seemed a long, long way from the old days, when she'd often seen Ernie setting the tiny separate letters in their frame, ready to print in black and white.

Soon the effort to understand was too much and she sat back and watched the changing expressions on Bart's face, the tiny lines of concentration between his dark brows, the way the keen blue eyes lit with enthusiasm as agreement was reached on some abstruse problem. She watched the way his long brown fingers curled round his pen as it flicked across the pages of his notebook, and her stomach churned as she had a treacherous memory of the way those same fingers had moved so tenderly across her breast.

Sometimes she thought she would go mad. Other times—mostly around three o'clock in the morning—she vowed to pull out of the whole affair of the partnership agreement before the final signing was done. But next morning Bart would walk in, fresh and groomed and smelling of his own brand of cologne, and she would know that she could never willingly go away where there was no chance of seeing him.

The few printing orders on hand had been executed and no new ones accepted. Ted had been put on paid leave to help his wife during her convalescence after the operation. It had been decided to start afresh 'with a bang', as Bart put it, when the company had been updated.

The first floor had been stripped and redecorated and would be used as a design studio. The large back room on the ground floor was to be the photographic department. The large front office had had a partition put up to make a reception area which opened off the hall, with an inner door which led, in turn, back into the main office. The decorating had been done, and the rest of the work, on Bart's insistence, was to be left for Philippa to arrange.

'You'll do it best,' he said. 'Curtains and carpets and so on. No expense spared.'

She smiled faintly. 'Women's work?'

He gave her a sharp glance. 'Not necessarily. There are surely as many good men interior designers as women. I don't happen to be one of them, that's all. And for heaven's sake don't waste time sniping at me, Philippa. We've got enough to do without that.'

She raised her brows. 'Haven't lost your sense of humour, have you?'

'Oh, shut up and get on with it.' He swung away and a moment later she heard him clattering down the basement stairs.

Well, well! This wasn't at all like the usually un-flappable Bart. Something had got into him. Perhaps his girlfriend was playing him up. Philippa had been trying painfully to train herself to live with the idea that surely, by now, he had acquired a girlfriend. What he had wanted from *her*—rather urgently—was merely a sexual liaison; he'd made that clear. When she'd refused him he'd doubtless found his satisfaction elsewhere.

She pushed the painful thought away and reached for a pad and pencil and immersed herself in planning. A few minutes later she heard the Jaguar start up outside. Bart had left without bothering to see her again, which was most unusual. She shrugged and tried not to care.

The following day he arrived in the late afternoon. He looked tired, as if he hadn't been sleeping. Philippa saw the dark lines under his eyes and felt a little tug at her heart, but merely said, 'Good afternoon, Bart,' and looked back to the papers before her on the desk.

He sank into a chair with a grunt of disgust. 'Bloody awful traffic on the motorway—I've been over an hour getting from Birmingham.'

'Too bad,' Philippa commiserated absently. If he wanted a drink he could get one himself. She wasn't his adoring secretary to rush to minister to his needs.

He got up, poured himself a whisky, and returned to his chair. After a few moments' silence, which seemed to Philippa to stretch unbearably, he said, 'Not sulking, are you?'

She looked up with an innocent smile. 'Why ever should you think that? Of course I'm not sulking—I'm rather involved in planning the new office, that's all.' She put down her pencil. 'Is there something you want to discuss?'

She must have convinced him. His expression relaxed. 'Several things. First, I've been with Robert most of the day. Everything signed, sealed and delivered. We seem to have come to the end of the planning process, so I'll leave you and Ernie in charge to get ahead here until I get back.'

'You're going away?'

'I'm off to New York tomorrow. I've been neglecting my own work recently and I must catch up.'

He'd been worrying about his work. Was that why he looked so tired and why he had snapped at her yesterday? Nothing to do with a girlfriend? Philippa clutched hopefully at the straw.

She said, 'We'll do our best.' She didn't know whether it would be a relief or a black misery not to have him dropping in every day. 'The new presses are due to be delivered next week, aren't they, but Ernie will supervise the installation, of course? I'll get on with the office renovation. That OK?'

'Of course,' he said absently. He picked up a Biro and fiddled with it, drawing a doodle on the scratchpad on the desk. Then he looked up, straight into her eyes. 'I rather hate the idea of going away when things are getting so interesting here.'

'But you have to?' She hated the idea too, but of course she couldn't say so.

'I'm afraid I do. The coffers have to be topped up.'

She said lightly, 'Another million in the bank?'

He grimaced. 'I'm not a millionaire, Philippa. Are you disappointed?'

'Of course not—it's nothing to do with me. I just thought . . .' she stopped awkwardly. Truth to tell, by the way he'd been pouring money into the Albany Press she'd imagined that he must be very rich indeed.

He frowned. 'I thought I'd told you. The money I'm putting into the business here has no connection with any of my other activities. My godmother, Tilly, left me a sizeable legacy, along with the cottage, and the wish that I'd use it for something I really cared about.' His face was suddenly grim. 'My ex-wife had the bright idea that I should invest it in her boutique, but I couldn't see the sense of that when...' He shrugged. 'Oh, well, that's all water under the bridge.'

There was a silence. Philippa wished he would go on, tell her something about his marriage and why he was so adamant that he wouldn't marry again, but instead he shook his head as if he was shaking off a bad memory, and went on practically, 'By the way, I think I've found us a secretary. Nice woman, in her forties. A widow, lives in Warwick. Name of Mary Walsh. She's coming over to see you at ten tomorrow morning; if you approve you could engage her to start immediately; she can be getting used to the place and she'll be useful to hold the fort if you want to be away from the office.'

Philippa nodded, jotting down the name. 'Have you settled on a salary?' When he mentioned a sum she wrote that down too. 'Right,' she said briskly. 'That all?'

He looked up at her then and the blue eyes were bleak, quite lacking their usual brilliance. 'Yes, that's all. Unless there's anything you want to tell me.'

Only that I love you.

'No, I don't think so,' she said crisply. 'Have a good trip. You'll be in touch?'

'I'll do my best, but I'll be moving around. If anything important comes up here, my secretary in Birmingham will probably know where I am. I've got a complicated assignment on. A British company based in the US. They're in quite a spot of trouble. It should be challenging.' He seemed to brighten slightly at the prospect.

'I'm sure you'll work miracles for them,' Philippa said.

He cast her a suspicious glance. 'We *are* being polite to each other today, aren't we, partner?' He got to his feet. 'Well, I'll be off home to get packing. See you when I get back. Be good, Philippa.'

For a moment he seemed to hesitate, almost as if he would come round the desk and take her hand or— or kiss her. A business kiss on the cheek, of course.

It was a relief that he didn't.

Mary Walsh appeared at ten o'clock prompt the following morning, and from the very first moment Philippa knew that they would get on together. She was plump and cheerful, with brown hair done up in a bun and soft brown eyes. She was forty-two, she told Philippa, and had been a widow for twelve years. She lived with her elderly mother in Warwick and she had been working as a temp in Bart's office in Birmingham.

'Mr Marchant knew I was looking for a job closer to home—the commuting takes up a lot of time and Mother gets very lonely. The Sprinter trains don't exactly sprint.' Her grin was humorously rueful. 'Mr Marchant remembered me when this job came up here. He's a boss who really considers his staff—very kind and understanding. But I expect you know that, Miss Price.'

Kind? Understanding? Bart? Well—yes, perhaps. But 'kind and understanding' weren't the first words she would apply to him. Philippa wondered, what *were* the first words? She'd have to think about that.

'I could start as soon as you like,' Mrs Walsh said eagerly. 'They will release me in Birmingham at any time.'

It was nice to make someone happy—and so easily too. 'I'd like you to start right away, Mrs Walsh,' Philippa said.

The brown eyes lit up. 'Oh, marvellous! And please call me Mary. But—don't you want to ask me questions? I've got a good typing speed—shorthand too, if you want it. I never gave up my job when I married. You see I—my husband Jim was...was delicate. He wasn't able to do regular work himself.' For a moment a shadow touched the cheerful face. 'I knew when we were married that I wouldn't have him very long.' She brightened. 'But we had six wonderful years together. We were so happy. It isn't everyone who can say that, is it?'

'Not everyone,' Philippa agreed. She admired Mary's positive approach to life. She herself would have to try harder to make the best of things. After all, she had the prospect of managing a thriving business. All right, she'd wanted to do it by herself, but she knew now that that hadn't been possible. She must accept Bart's help gracefully, co-operate fully, and put her personal emotions in the background. By the time he returned from New York, she vowed, he would find her much easier to get along with.

She pushed back her chair and stood up. 'Would you like to take off your coat and have a look round, Mary? I can explain about the alterations we're going to make and introduce you to the men down in the printing shop. Then we'll have coffee and talk over what we'll do to start with. I'd like to get the place refurbished by the time Mr Marchant gets back from New York.'

And get myself refurbished too, she added silently. Bart would see a difference in her, as well as in the office, when he got back. She was going to work on it.

And work on it she did.

On the day after the new carpets had been laid and the new curtains fitted she said to Mary—who had quickly become a friend as well as a secretary—'Would you be a dear and hold the fort for me this afternoon while I go out shopping? I've decided that the time has come to smarten myself up. Everything else is changing around here, so why not me?'

'I think you're very nice as you are,' Mary told her comfortably. 'But I know exactly how you feel. You go ahead, and I'll cope with anything that turns up.'

So Philippa took her credit card and went shopping for clothes that would confirm her new image as a confident young career-woman. First she chose a suit in fine pearly-grey wool. White blouses in wild silk with a feminine touch of frilliness at neck and cuffs. Sheer tights. Black kid pumps with a slim briefcase to match. Two skirts for wear in the office—one a pleated little number in a plum colour, the other straight and slim in clear emerald-green. The white blouses would go with these when the warmer weather came. Meanwhile she chose a couple of crew-neck jumpers, also in white. She deliberately avoided anything in violet and tried not to think about the shawl Bart had given her.

Off-duty clothes would have to wait. She didn't expect to go out much in the evenings anyway, and she was near the limit of her credit card.

She hesitated over the final touch before she made up her mind, thought about it over a cup of tea in the store restaurant, and eventually took the plunge and made her way to the hairdressing department. Here she put herself in the hands of a smart young woman who proved interested and sympathetic. She walked round Philippa, surveying her head from all angles, and finally recommended a short cut.

Philippa took a deep breath and agreed, but she had to close her eyes when the weight of her silky dark tresses fell to the floor and she felt the scissors snipping coldly against her neck. After the shampoo she was sure she'd made a terrible mistake; she looked, she decided, like the proverbial drowned rat. But when the blow-dry was completed and the hairdresser held up a mirror for Philippa's inspection she turned her head this way and that and knew that the result was just the effect she had wanted. The dark, feathery cap bounced cheekily as the hairdresser ran skilful fingers through it. For the first time in her life, Philippa thought delightedly, she no longer looked submissive and biddable—wimpish was the word that came into her mind: she looked cool, confident and efficient— a young woman who had taken her life in her own hands. Not aggressive but assertive—that was the right word. She went out into the street, carrying her bags and parcels, with a new light in her big grey eyes. Bart was going to get quite a surprise when he next saw her.

He strolled into the office one afternoon, three weeks later, as casually as if he'd never been away. Mary had already left and Philippa was working late on staff insurance and PAYE.

Her heart gave a heavy throb and seemed to beat in her throat as she looked up from her desk and saw him open the door. His dress was informal; he wore tight black trousers and an open-necked blue shirt, with a loose black jacket over it, and the sight of him almost played havoc with her composure, but somehow she managed to feign cool surprise and no more.

'I'm back,' he said. There was a half-smile on his mouth as he studied her face thoroughly.

'So I see.' Her answering smile was cool and pleasant. It had to be like this because if she allowed him to guess the crazy happiness that was running like a warm tide through her body it would undo all the work she'd been doing on herself during his absence. 'I didn't think you'd be in until tomorrow. Louise rang from Birmingham to say you were expected back there today.'

He was standing beside the desk, hands in pockets, still with his eyes fixed on her face. 'I came straight from the airport. I couldn't get here quickly enough.'

She wished he would move or look away or something. The dark blue stare was throwing her into confusion.

Her laugh sounded forced. 'You couldn't wait to see your new acquisition?'

'Of course,' he said, with a touch of irony she couldn't account for. 'What have you done to your hair?'

'I've had it cut—I needed a change.' She didn't ask him if he liked it. 'Look around you and you'll notice quite a few other changes.'

She got to her feet because she couldn't sit there looking up at him any longer, meeting those un-wavering eyes that seemed to be a deeper blue than before. 'Mary Walsh and I have been very busy spending your money while you've been away. We've been going round the sales. I don't know what you think, but I liked the idea of keeping the Regency style in this office. Somehow it didn't seem right to present a high-tech appearance. We bought the chairs and the davenport at a sale in an old manor house near Banbury. We had fun—I've never been to a sale before, but Mary showed me the ropes and in the end I was bidding like an old hand.' She was jabbering and she knew it, but the sudden, unexpected sight of Bart had made her fizz inside like a bottle of cham-pagne which had had its cork knocked off. 'Mary is an absolute treasure and such a nice person. We get on extremely well . . .'

He reached out and put a hand on her arm and she felt herself shiver. 'I'm glad,' he said quietly. 'I'll look at it all afterwards. I was hoping you'd offer me the solace of a quiet drink up in your flat. Air travel always leaves me whacked.'

'Of course,' she said immediately. 'How thoughtless of me.' She switched off the desk lamp and led the way upstairs. She wondered if he noticed the new carpet on the stairs, but probably he didn't. He was obviously too tired to notice anything very much, and that prolonged stare he had turned on her when he had first come in hadn't meant a thing, other than that he was fagged out.

Up in the flat he sank down on to the sofa with a grunt of satisfaction and leaned his head back. She gave him a whisky and went into the kitchen to make coffee.

'Have you eaten?' she asked, putting her head round the door.

'Not since breakfast. I can never eat on a plane.'

'How about an omelette with baked beans?'

'Sounds marvellous,' he said, and yawned.

Philippa went back into the kitchen, opened a tin of beans and whipped up four eggs thoughtfully. She'd never seen Bart looking tired before. He'd always been very much aware and awake. It presented a different side of him—a vulnerable, intimate side which played havoc with her determination to forget any personal relationship between them. The last thing she needed was to let herself feel maternal towards him. She could imagine how he'd turn a shaft of sarcasm on to her.

The omelette turned out satisfactorily fluffy. She arranged the beans beside it, carried the tray into the living-room and put it down on the low table by the sofa. Bart had drained his glass and was lying back with his eyes closed.

'Food,' Philippa announced loudly, in case he had dropped off to sleep.

He didn't stir.

'Bart—wake up, your omelette will be cold.' She gripped his arm and shook it briskly.

His other hand came out and closed round her wrist and she found herself pulled down on the sofa beside him.

'What was that about a flask of wine...loaf of bread...and thou...?' he muttered sleepily, and gathered her against him.

Her senses swam. 'Bart—wake up,' she shouted close to his ear.

He nuzzled his mouth into her neck. 'Don't want to...wake up.'

His face was so close. She could see the fine lines round his eyes, the way his mouth curved, the pinpoints of dark hair on his chin. But nothing had changed, of course; he was merely rambling on out of sheer tiredness. She longed to relax against him, to rub her cheek against the roughness of his chin, but that would never do. One thing would lead to another and she would be lost.

With a tremendous effort, she twisted away from him and stood up again. 'Do you want to eat or don't you?' she said very loudly.

He opened his eyes then and stared at her glassily. 'Philippa! I thought I'd gone to heaven and met an angel.' He pulled himself up with an effort.

She stood looking down at him, hands on hips. 'Don't be ridiculous. Now, eat up the nice omelette that Nanny has made for you.'

He gave her his lop-sided grin. 'Nanny be blowed,' he said. 'But it looks very good, I must say.' He picked up his fork and she felt that the danger was over—for the moment.

He put down his coffee-cup with a long sigh ten minutes later. 'That was delicious. You know, Philippa, this place is beginning to feel like home to me. Do you mind?'

'I don't mind at all,' she said briskly, picking up the tray. 'I'm glad to provide a modest meal at any time.'

He sighed again. 'That wasn't quite what I meant. But no matter. OK, let's go down again and you can show me all you've been doing.'

Down in the office he looked round quickly and approved of everything. 'I like the idea of keeping it all in period. I agree that modern executive-type furniture wouldn't look right in this room. The blue cord carpet's a good choice, and the curtain pattern is definitely William Morris. We keep the modern stuff next door, in Mary's office, is that the idea?'

Philippa nodded. 'Yes, that's the idea.' She felt rather disappointed with his almost careless acceptance of all her hard work. She supposed she'd been silly to expect anything more enthusiastic, but she told herself that he was tired, and anyway this was business—she shouldn't expect compliments on doing her job.

She hesitated at the door that led down to the basement. 'Do you want to see the printing shop too? Or would you rather wait until Ernie's here to show it to you? The new presses were installed last Friday— they look very smart, and Ernie's over the moon.'

'I'd like *you* to show them to me,' Bart said quietly and followed her down the stairs.

She switched on the three new overhead fluorescent strips, and the basement was flooded with white light. 'Quite a transformation, don't you think?' Philippa said brightly. Bart was standing close to her and his nearness was disturbing her. She moved away and said, 'Ernie's been giving me quite a bit of instruction on the work we can turn out, so that I'll be able to talk intelligently to the customers, but I've got a great deal more to learn about the design side.'

Bart was following her round, keeping much too close behind her for her own comfort. She said quickly, 'The old Albion press is still here, of course, in the next room.' She led the way through a door into the big back room. 'We put everything here that belongs to it—all the cabinets and the old composing table and so on. Is that what you wanted?'

She turned to him for confirmation and caught her breath. He wasn't looking at the heavy press, he was looking at her, and there was an unnerving hunger in his blue eyes. 'It wasn't all I wanted,' he said softly.

She could feel her eyes widening. They seemed to cling to his and couldn't move. For a moment the old feeling of weakness when confronted with a stronger personality almost took over. She only had to smile at him, to move closer...

He put both his hands on her shoulders but he didn't attempt to draw her against him. He said, 'I haven't given up, you know, Philippa. I still think our partnership shouldn't be limited to office hours. I've thought about it a lot while I've been away.' His voice deepened, roughened. 'I want you very much, little girl. I'm sorry to keep on and on about it, but I don't seem to be able to get you out of my system.'

She had thought about it too, while he'd been away, and her resolution hadn't changed. She'd half expected that this would happen and she had rehearsed her answer. If he'd said he loved her, needed her, she would have gone into his arms joyfully. But all he wanted was a sexual release and that wasn't enough. When his physical need for her had waned, what would she be left with? She wasn't made like Chloe, who would easily pass on to the next man. She thought perhaps that she was out of place in this modern world of casual sex.

She moved back so that his hands fell away, and said, 'My feelings haven't changed, Bart. I don't think it would be a good idea. I'm sure we'd both enjoy it—and it would be very convenient for you to use my flat whenever you felt like a spot of dalliance. But it's not what I've got in mind for the way I want my life to go.'

His dark brows went up and he said, almost with a sneer, 'And how *do* you want your life to go, Philippa? I thought you were keen on a career—on managing a business. You can't combine that with a little home for two and a couple of children playing on the lawn. It never works. But if you don't acknowledge your normal sexual urges you'll turn into a dried-up middle-aged female.' His mouth was a hard line and his eyes were as cold as the ocean.

She glared at him and said, 'If you're accusing me of holding out for marriage, it isn't true and I resent it.'

'You're all mixed up, Philippa. I'm not accusing you of anything but being a wrong-minded little——' He grabbed her round the waist and pulled her towards him, and his mouth came down on hers with a terrible frustrated urgency. One arm clamped her against him and the other hand went to the buttons of her blouse and ripped them apart, pulling away the wisp of lace and satin beneath. His mouth moved down her neck and closed hungrily over the peak of her breast. Her senses swam and her body went limp in his arms. For a treacherous moment she ached to respond, to move against him in a frenzied need to match his own. But only for a moment. Then the words seemed to form themselves in her head. I won't give in. I won't, I won't let him take me like this, and she was pushing him away, fighting to be free.

'Stop it, Bart,' she gasped. 'Stop it. You've no right...'

He let her go immediately and turned away, breathing heavily. 'Sorry, Philippa, sorry,' he muttered over his shoulder, his voice ragged.

She was leaning weakly against the heavy old press, and a protruding part of it was sticking into her back as she fumbled with the buttons of her blouse. She wondered if her legs would take her to the stairs and up to the office. At the moment they felt useless.

Bart turned back to her slowly. 'Of course I've got no right. It's just that... Oh, hell, I don't know. I've never felt so like rape before. I suppose the fact that I've been celibate for so long has got to me. Look, can we forget it?' He gave her the ghost of his usual laid-back smile. 'We'll make a good job of being business partners, shall we? And I promise not to encourage any other ideas to take root in my mind.' He held out his hand. 'Partners?'

'Partners,' she replied, putting her hand in his. He gripped it hard for a brief moment and then let his hand fall heavily to his side. 'I'd better remove myself from the premises. I'll come in tomorrow and talk to Ernie about the new set-up.' He waved a hand vaguely towards the new presses in the adjoining room.

Philippa struggled for normality. 'Have you got your car here?'

'Yes. I parked it while I was away with some friends who live near Heathrow.' He gave her an odd little grin. 'It's all right, I promise not to go berserk on the way home.'

She followed him up the stairs to the hall, where he picked up his bag and travelling coat.

'Goodnight—partner,' he said. He went out and slammed the front door behind him.

'Goodnight, my love,' Philippa whispered. She had won a battle—with herself, not with him, but the victory felt very, very hollow.

CHAPTER NINE

A WEEK later, on Wednesday, a staff meeting was called. 'I'll take the chair, shall I, or would you rather do it?' Bart asked Philippa in advance.

She glanced up from her desk and said, 'Would it be a good idea for you to chair the first meeting and I'll take the next one?' That way she could watch how it was done.

'Right,' he agreed. So at five o'clock the four of them were sitting round the office as Bart opened the proceedings.

Philippa watched and listened, and as the meeting went on she learned quite a lot about Bart, as well as about the way to chair a staff meeting.

This was his job—business management—and she had to admit he was brilliant at it. She saw the way Ernie and Mary lost their first stiff nervousness and opened out under his skilful guidance. Their tentative suggestions were listened to carefully, and somehow Bart managed to make them feel that Ernie's request for a tea-machine and Mary's leaking radiator in the office were of prime importance to him.

He even managed to fit in a small compliment to Philippa herself. 'My congratulations on the Press release for the local papers, Philippa; you've done a splendid job. It was a good idea of yours to let them know what we were starting up.'

Bart certainly knew how to make friends and influence people, she thought. What a difference from

Father's bad old days! If only he had realised, as Bart appeared to do, that you got the best out of people when you didn't bully them. She watched Bart's serious, interested face as he discussed various small points with the other two. Was this merely his business persona, she wondered, his clever way of manipulating people, or was he a really nice, sincere man?

She was so deep in thought that she gave a start when Bart looked round and asked crisply, 'Any other business? No? That concludes the proceedings, then; we'll meet again next week. Thank you all for coming.'

Ernie and Mary departed by their separate exits and Bart pulled his chair up to the desk, facing Philippa.

'Well,' he said, with his enigmatic smile, 'do you feel any happier now about accepting the new situation? It seems to me that things couldn't be more satisfactory.'

She evaded the question. 'I certainly know more about the printing business. I might even be able to talk the right language to customers soon—now that I've been learning from Ernie about the working of the new presses. That was what you told me to do, wasn't it?'

The smile disappeared. Obviously he suspected sarcasm. 'What I *suggested*—yes.'

Across the desk their glances met and, for a moment, challenged each other. A ripple of excitement touched Philippa's stomach. She was learning, quite quickly, to hold her own.

Bart got up and walked to the window, looking out across the shadowy trees in the square. 'Talking of customers,' he said, 'I've been liaising with Pargeter's editor quite a bit recently—a bright girl, name of Madeleine Clark. She's very interested in our new venture. I think she'll probably be helpful in putting a good deal of business our way—the kind of thing we want.'

'Oh, yes?' Philippa felt a sharp stab of pain behind her ribs as she wondered if he had been wining and dining the bright Ms Clark in the interest of new business. In one way she wanted to believe that he had. If she managed to despise him just a little, perhaps she wouldn't love him so much. But the idea of Bart and the unknown Ms Clark together made her feel slightly sick and she pushed it away quickly.

'By the way, Philippa, John Pargeter wants to come over and have a look at us, and bring Madeleine with him. I'll have to arrange that.' He stood up, glancing at his watch. 'I'll be off now. I've got a date this evening. I shan't be in tomorrow. Ring me at the office if anything turns up. I'll look in Friday afternoon—lateish, probably.'

'Right,' Philippa said, pulling a heavy ledger towards her. 'Goodnight, Bart.'

'Night, partner.' He went out and closed the door.

She stared down at the book blindly. Suddenly depression settled over her, as it had been doing more and more frequently lately. How much longer, she wondered, could she go on like this, loving him so much, seeing him almost every day, but with this barrier of polite indifference separating them? It was almost too much to bear, and two fat tears gathered in her eyes and rolled down her cheeks.

She was berating herself for weakness, fumbling for a handkerchief, when the phone rang on her desk.

'Hello, Pippa, darling, it's me.' Chloe was bubbling with excitement. 'Can't talk long, I'm up to my eyes in work, trying to get everything straight before my wedding *next Tuesday . . .*' She paused for the announcement to sink in.

'*Chloe*—so soon?' Philippa squeaked.

'It surprised me too,' Chloe said. 'What's happened is that Claude has had some order or other put off for a month so he's got a week free. I've managed to clear the same week, so off we go to the jolly old town hall next Tuesday at twelve. Now you must come over on Monday at the latest—sooner if you can. I've posted off your tickets to make sure you do. You should get them tomorrow. OK?'

Philippa tried to get her breath back. 'Yes, very much OK. I'm dying to meet Claude. I've got hundreds of questions to ask, but I can't think of any of them—my head's spinning. Is it going to be a big "do", and what should I wear?'

'No, a very quiet "do". And wear anything you like, darling. I'm not dressing up—I'll be wearing the outfit I'm travelling in. We'll be leaving for Claude's house in Provence after the wedding. Just a small buffet lunch in Claude's apartment, with Henri, Claude's brother, and a few friends. Henri is Pascal's father—he and his wife are separated. You know Pascal, of course.' Her voice became teasing as she added, 'He can't wait to see you again—you made a hit there, Sis.'

'That's nice,' said Philippa. 'But don't start getting ideas, Chloe. I'm not . . .' Her voice trailed off.

There was a little silence, then Chloe said, 'There's something going on, isn't there? I can tell by your voice. What's up, Pippa? It's not this new man, is it—this Bartholomew individual? Is he getting you down?'

Getting me down? He's got me down, Philippa thought bleakly. Down, and out for the count. 'I'm OK,' she said. 'Things are a bit mixed up just now— I'll tell you when I see you.' She changed the subject. 'Is Robert coming?' she enquired cautiously. She didn't particularly want to encounter Robert again just at present.

She heard Chloe's light, gurgling laugh. 'Brother Robert? Oh, dear me, no. When I rang him just now he was quite shirty about it. Said I should have informed him earlier—as if I could! He can't possibly get away at such short notice, it would be *most* inconvenient. He said he wished me happiness and is sending a small cheque. I think we can do without Robert—we're likely to be a merry party and he'd be rather a skeleton at the feast, poor Robert! Bye for now, ducky. I'll ring on Sunday to finalise arrangements.'

It was almost six o'clock when Bart arrived on Friday afternoon. He looked tired, but refused Philippa's polite offer of coffee. 'A heavy day,' he said. 'All I want to do is to get home and into a shower and then see what the invaluable Mrs McLeod has provided for supper. You must come to supper again one day, Philippa,' he added in an offhand way. 'The woman's turning out to be a marvel.'

'Thank you,' Philippa said rather woodenly, remembering the last time she had been in his cottage and how it had started the sequence of events that had followed so quickly. How she had believed then that he was beginning to fall in love with her, and what an idiot she had been. Just thinking about it made her cringe.

'Everything OK here?' Bart asked. He didn't sit down, but stood beside the desk, not looking at her.

'Fine,' she said. 'I've had a good many replies in to our advertisement for a computer designer. Perhaps you'd like to take them with you, to go through at your leisure.' She handed over a wad of letters.

He stuffed them into his briefcase. 'Thanks. Oh, and I wanted to tell you—I've arranged with a surveyor friend of mine to come and look over the house. It seems to me that the exterior's in quite a bad state. His name's Barker, and he'll ring you to make a convenient appointment. That OK?'

Philippa bit her lip to stop herself telling him that he didn't own the whole house, but she knew that the details had still to be settled with the solicitors, who were taking their time about producing the partnership agreement, and she supposed that what he suggested was reasonable. 'OK,' she said, nodding briefly.

'And another thing,' Bart went on, 'I've invited John Pargeter to come over here next Monday and bring Madeleine with him. I thought you and Mary might put your heads together and provide some snacks—I'll lay on drinks.'

'Yes, I'll...' She broke off. 'Oh, no, I'm sorry, I can't manage Monday.'

'Why not?' he said sharply.

'I've made other arrangements. I'm flying to Paris on Monday.'

'Paris!' Suddenly his face changed, the blue eyes grew frosty. 'What the hell do you want to go to Paris for?'

It should have been easy to say 'I'm going over for my sister's wedding. The date's been put forward unexpectedly', but she didn't intend to justify or make excuses. 'A social engagement,' she replied distantly.

'It's very inconvenient,' he snapped. 'You should have told me before. I'll look a fool if I have to cancel with Pargeter. Can't you put your *social* visit off until later?'

She shook her head. 'I'm sorry,' she said again, ignoring the sneer in his voice.

'You're sorry,' he barked. 'Don't you know the first thing about a partnership yet? You don't go swanning off abroad to enjoy yourself without at least consulting with your partner about dates.'

'You didn't consult me about this Pargeter thing,' she came back at him, grey eyes stormy.

'That's different—that's important. We need Pargeter's goodwill to get the new business started. We can't afford to dither and give the impression we're not reliable. You should have asked me before you made this Paris arrangement.'

He was white with anger, just as Father would have been if she'd done something he objected to. But she wasn't going to allow Bart Marchant to bully her. This was just the kind of situation she'd vowed never to let herself be sucked into again.

She managed to keep admirably calm. She said, 'Have you heard when the partnership papers will be ready for us to sign?'

'Next week, I believe.' He gave her a sharp look. 'Why?'

'Because,' she said slowly, 'if this is going to be your general attitude I certainly wouldn't put up with it and I may as well back out now.'

'Don't be so ridiculous.' He waved that away impatiently. 'You can't.' He slapped a hand down on his desk.

'Oh, but I can,' she said, and managed a faint smile. 'Nobody can make me sign my name if I don't choose to.'

He breathed heavily in silence as if struggling for patience. Then at last he said, 'OK, you win. Leave a phone number with Mary where you can be reached. When will you be back?'

'I'm not sure. Wednesday or Thursday probably.'

'Well, let me know as soon as you arrive,' he said wearily, 'so that I can make another date with Pargeter.'

'Of course,' she said, keeping her voice steady with an effort.

He got to his feet, looking down at her with an expression she couldn't interpret—except that it wasn't exactly anger. 'I think, Philippa,' he said with slow deliberation, 'that I'd rather like to wring your neck. Goodnight.'

It was some time before Philippa's limbs stopped shaking. Disagreeable scenes had always had this effect on her and she acknowledged that it was a weakness. So many times she should have stood up to Father and had given in for the sake of peace.

But this time she hadn't given in; she had stood her ground and made her point. Somehow, though, there was no satisfaction in having won the argument. She didn't enjoy fighting, and probably she never would. But I shall have to get much, much tougher, she told herself, if I am to be a successful businesswoman.

She didn't want to think about that now, though, she wanted to think about Chloe and her news and the delightful prospect of a trip to Paris. She closed the office and went up to her flat to plan in detail the clothes she would take with her.

On Saturday morning Philippa phoned Mary, at home. 'I'm going off to France rather unexpectedly on Monday, Mary. Sorry to give you such short notice, but I didn't know myself until just after the meeting. Can you cope with anything that turns up? Yes, I'm sure you can. You've got your own key and I'll leave a note of my phone number on the desk. I'll ring and let you know when I'm coming back.'

Deliberately she didn't tell Mary about the wedding. Mary might quite easily mention it to Bart, and for some obscure reason Philippa didn't want Bart to know. Her private life was her own and Bart must be kept out of it.

Mary assured her that she would take charge of the office with pleasure. 'Have a nice time,' she said. 'I hope it's lovely weather for you in Paris.'

The airline tickets arrived on Saturday and Philippa began to have a pleasant feeling of anticipation. She cleared up a few loose ends in the office and then went to the shops to search for a wedding present for Chloe. She chose a small, rather beautiful crystal vase. It seemed to be just right for Chloe, as it sparkled and glittered in the overhead lights.

Pleased with her purchase, she treated herself to coffee in the store restaurant and pondered about clothes. The grey suit was quite smart but, worn with a white blouse, it didn't seem very festive. But a whole new outfit was out of the question. She'd already spent almost up to the limit on her credit card, and until the details of the partnership were agreed she had no idea what income she might expect from the business.

Finally she chose a filmy blouse in palest pink chiffon, with very full draped sleeves. It would look good with the pearl-grey of the suit, and if any evening 'occasion' had been planned she could wear the skirt and top without the coat, and feel suitably dressed.

On Sunday she tidied the flat, busied herself washing everything in sight, including her hair, and then took a long, leisurely time packing her hand luggage, congratulating herself that she'd only now and again thought about Bart. He'd been such a pig about her going away, why should she let her foolish infatuation for him—that was how she was trying to think of it—spoil such a wonderful, exciting occasion as Chloe's wedding? She would put him out of her mind for three whole days and really enjoy herself.

There was one thing about Paris, Philippa decided on Monday afternoon when she arrived there—everything seemed to whiz round so fast that one's spirits vibrated in sympathy.

Chloe met her at Charles de Gaulle Airport and hugged her enthusiastically, exuding a delicate cloud of French perfume. 'Pippa—you look marvellous. I love your new hairstyle. You look——' she stood back and surveyed her sister at arm's length '—quite different.'

Philippa grimaced. 'There was room for improvement, don't you think?'

Chloe wrinkled her nose. 'I rather liked my little sister as she was. I'll have to get used to this elegant young executive!'

Philippa laughed. 'I'm just the same inside.'

'Oh, no, you're not.' Chloe shook her head in disbelief. 'Something's happened, and you'll have to tell me about it later on. We'll go into town first—I've still got a spot of shopping to do. I have to pick up my outfit for tomorrow—the skirt's being shortened slightly—and then we'll go back to the apartment and have a lovely cosy chat. We're meeting Claude and Henri and Pascal for dinner. Come along, I'll find a taxi.'

And Philippa was whisked away.

It was five o'clock by the time they arrived at Chloe's apartment on the leafy outskirts of Paris, in a taxi spilling over with boxes and bags in rainbow colours, with the names of famous Paris stores splashed across them.

Chloe pulled her shoes off with a sigh of relief and padded across the living-room to the kitchen. 'I never knew getting married was so exhausting,' she declared happily, putting the kettle on to boil. 'Make yourself at home, darling. Take your things into the spare bedroom—you know where it is.'

Philippa had braved Father's disapproval and spent a weekend here when Chloe had first moved into the apartment two years ago, and now she looked round with pleased recognition. The apartment was so like Chloe herself: subtly elegant, but with a touch of fun here and there—from the scarlet cushions on the pink sofa to the large porcelain doll's head on the secretaire.

'Are you admiring my doll?' Chloe said, coming in with the tea-tray. 'She's quite old; she once had a rag body, but it must have fallen to bits ages ago, poor thing. I found her at the flea market. Claude and I had a fun afternoon there a while ago. Now come and sit down and we'll have a natter.'

A buzzer sounded in the hall and she got up with a groan to answer it. A minute or two later she came back into the living-room with a tall, extremely good-looking man beside her.

'This,' said Chloe, 'is Claude. The wretched man says he couldn't wait any longer to inspect you, Pippa. Claude, *chéri*, meet my baby sister.'

A pair of wicked dark eyes laughed into Philippa's and she was kissed warmly on both cheeks. '*Enchanté*,' murmured Claude, and looked as if he really meant it.

The wedding present was unpacked and exclaimed over with delight and placed beside the doll's head, and Philippa was thanked and kissed by the happy couple. Plans for the next day were finalised, and there was certainly no opportunity for a cosy chat with Chloe, for which Philippa was thankful. The last thing she wanted to do was to let her own troubles intrude on her sister's happiness.

The remainder of that day passed so pleasantly that she could almost forget them herself—except when she caught the intimate glances exchanged between her sister and her husband-to-be, so full of love and promise.

Dinner was at a small restaurant which Philippa guessed was famous for its cuisine. Henri, Claude's brother, had a fund of amusing stories from his travels as representative of a wine-making firm, and from the moment the small party gathered together at a candlelit table in an alcove he took charge of the conversation, grimacing horribly at his English, which, in truth, was excellent. And Pascal, who joined the party later, insisted on moving everyone round so that he could sit next to Philippa, and flattered her outrageously.

After dinner Pascal was all for going on to a nightclub, but Claude vetoed the idea. 'We shall all have an early night,' he decreed. 'Don't forget, we have a wedding tomorrow,' and his brother added some remark in French, which Philippa couldn't understand, but which set the rest of the party laughing immoderately.

It was close on midnight when Chloe and Philippa were finally alone in the apartment. 'A pot of tea before we go to bed, I think,' Chloe said. 'After all that food and wine we need a refresher.'

'Oh, it was lovely,' Philippa sighed, following her into the kitchen. 'I can't ever remember enjoying myself so much. Claude is a darling, and Henri and Pascal are such delightful people. They made me feel as if I were—sort of one of the family.'

'I'm very lucky,' Chloe said quietly as they settled down together in the living-room, and her eyes were suddenly misty. 'I never thought I'd want to exchange my free-wheeling ways to become part of a real family, but—one changes, you know.'

'Do you still plan to keep your job?' Philippa asked.

'Oh, yes—until a baby comes along. Possibly not even then; we'll have to see.'

Chloe with a baby! Philippa grinned, shaking her head. 'I haven't got used to the idea of a domesticated sister yet. Last time we were together you were all for arranging your love-life as a series of affairs. You almost convinced me that was the sensible way... but...' Her voice trailed off.

There was a small silence. Then Chloe put down her cup and said, 'Now—out with it, Pippa, I want to know what's going on with this Bartholomew individual.'

Philippa gasped and the blood ran hotly into her cheeks. 'There isn't anything...' she began. 'Well...how did you know?' she finished helplessly.

Her sister smiled fondly. 'My sweet, I almost brought you up, you know, and I haven't known you for twenty-one years without recognising the signs. Come on, out with it.'

There was no way of hiding anything from Chloe in this mood. So Philippa gave her an edited version of her meeting and subsequent relationship with Bart, leaving out everything that would seem to put him in a bad light. It was perhaps foolish, but she felt it would be a kind of betrayal to talk of that to anyone, even Chloe.

'In a nutshell, then,' Chloe said, after a long pause for thought, 'he wanted an affair, but you wouldn't go along with it. Why, Pippa?'

'I told you,' Philippa said miserably. 'I'm in love with him, but he's not in love with me. He only wants to go to bed with me.'

Chloe said very gently, 'If you love the man, don't hold back, Sis. It could turn out for you as it's done for me.'

'You mean—he might decide he wants to marry me?' She shook her head. 'Not a hope!'

'Rubbish! Where there's love, there's always hope— to coin a phrase. Anyway, what have you got to lose, Pippa? You wouldn't be any worse off than you are now. Which is pretty dire, my sweet, by the look of you.'

'Oh, I would, I would,' Philippa wailed. 'If we had an affair and it finished when he got tired of me I think I'd die.'

'Rubbish again,' Chloe scoffed. 'Now, promise me that when you get back you'll follow your heart, not your head. You're not the hard-boiled type, little sister, and when you're in love you've got to take a risk. Goodness, I *am* full of clichés today—but the funny thing about clichés is that they're usually true.'

Philippa looked at her doubtfully. 'And what happens when it all goes wrong? I couldn't stay on being Bart's partner after... after...' She bit her lip.

'Sell him the rest of the company, love, and come over here to us. I'll find you a job.'

'You make it sound so easy.' Philippa had to smile, but the smile was rather crooked. 'Now, that's enough of me and my miseries. You go along and get your beauty sleep; I'll wash these things up. And—thanks for the advice, Chloe. I'll think about it.' She tried to sound practical and unemotional, but she didn't think her sister was deceived.

Chloe reached out and touched her cheek. 'You're a dear, sweet girl, Pippa. And if this Bart man hurts you I'll come over and sort him out myself,' she added fiercely.

They laughed together, and there were tears behind the laughter.

The wedding-day unreeled itself before Philippa's wondering eyes like a colour film: driving in a taxi to the town hall along the wide sunny boulevards; watching Chloe and Claude making their vows— Chloe looking beautiful and calm in a designer suit of thick aubergine-colour silk, and Claude, handsome and debonair, and quite unable to take his eyes off his new wife; the buffet lunch in Claude's luxury apartment by the river; the buzz of unintelligible talk which rose to a babble as more and more guests drifted in from their cars; the colours of the banked flowers, the smell of perfume; the champagne that tickled her nose when the toasts were drunk; it was all bewildering and wonderful and quite unlike anything that had happened to her before.

She was aware that Pascal was staying close beside her through it all, so that she never felt left out. When Claude and Chloe were ready to leave for their three-hundred-kilometre drive Philippa had a few moments alone with Chloe.

'It's all been wonderful,' Philippa said chokily as she helped her sister adjust the posy of pink carnations on her shoulder. 'Have a lovely time.'

'Thank you, Sis, we will.' Chloe grinned wickedly. 'You'll be OK in the apartment tonight, won't you? Pascal will look after you, and Henri has instructed him to be on his best behaviour. Henri would stay himself but he has to leave straight away for Lille, where he's supposed to be at a conference.' She kissed Philippa. 'Be good, little sister, and I hope to hear some cheerful news from you very soon.'

When the farewells were over and the rice had been thrown after the departing car Henri was next to leave, kissing Philippa on both cheeks and insisting that she should come back soon.

After that the guests all drifted away until only Pascal and Philippa were left. She had a sudden pang of loneliness. It had been such a wonderful, happy time, and now she had to go back and face a very uncertain and unpromising future.

She sighed, watching Pascal rescuing the remainder of a plate of canapés from one of the catering staff, who had moved in to begin tidying up.

He offered her the plate. 'A pity to waste excellent food,' he grinned.

She shook her head. 'No thanks. I'd better be getting back to Chloe's apartment. I have to make an early start to the airport in the morning.'

Pascal looked horrified. 'Mais non! *Non, pas question*! I have made plans for this evening. I have looked forward ever since we met in Leamington.'

Pascal had been a little subdued in the company of his urbane, witty father, but now he had Philippa to himself he came out of his shell.

'*Ecoutez*!' he announced masterfully. 'We go for a stroll beside the river and see the sun set. Then we take a little drive round Paris and I show you what you call the "sights". Afterwards, perhaps, if you are not tired, we go on to a little place where we can dance. And at the end I take you back to your apartment and see that you are safe for the night. In the morning I call for you and take you to the airport. *Alors*, how is that?' he finished triumphantly.

She laughed. 'Pascal! You are suddenly very masterful.'

He winked. 'Ah, earlier I do not wish to steal my father's—how do you say?—steal my father's lightning.'

She laughed. 'Thunder.'

'*Oui*, thunder. How do you like my plan?'

'Sounds lovely.' He was very sweet, Philippa thought. The least she could do was to make the evening pleasurable for him, and the obvious way to do that was to enjoy every moment of it herself.

It wasn't difficult to do just that.

The evening was surprisingly warm for March, and they strolled hand in hand along the riverbank and watched the lights come on. The trees were still bare and Pascal insisted that Philippa must come back in April when it was green and leafy. 'But you are per'aps getting cold, so now we drive.'

Taxis seemed to appear from nowhere when Pascal summoned them. A round-tour of the city left Philippa dazed with an impression of gaiety and swirling cars, and the crowds strolling in the warm of the evening. They swept quickly past cafés and restaurants and huge, whitely lit shop windows that lined the wide boulevards. The Eiffel Tower reared its elegant floodlit slimness into a sky where the stars were almost dimmed by the brilliance below, and in the Place de la Concorde the spotlights played on buildings and monuments, and turned the fountain into a cascade of sparkling silver.

'Beautiful!' sighed Philippa when the taxi halted outside what appeared to be the entrance to a theatre.

'And now I have a leetle surprise for you,' Pascal announced.

The 'leetle surprise' turned out to be tickets for a musical show at one of Paris's small, intimate theatres. 'You're spoiling me,' Philippa declared as they came out into the glittering boulevard two hours later. 'I did so enjoy it—it was so... so light-hearted and happy.'

Pascal beamed with pleasure and consulted his watch. 'It is too early to end the evening yet—we shall go to a club that I know, and dance. Yes?'

He pleaded so nicely and, truth to tell, Philippa didn't want the day to end yet, so she was whisked away in another taxi.

They sat at a table for two covered by a red and white check cloth and drank more champagne, watched the floor show and danced to smoochy music; Pascal held her close in the dim light and rested his cheek against her hair, and Philippa felt that Paris was a sort of out-of-this-world wonderland that soothed away all your worries.

But at last Pascal said regretfully, 'Now it is past midnight and Cinderella must go home. Chloe has trusted me to look after you. It is very hard to be so good, but I must keep my promise.'

A taxi took them back to Chloe's apartment. 'I have the key and I will see you safe,' he said, summoning the lift.

The phone was ringing as they opened the door of the apartment. Pascal chuckled. 'It is Chloe, checking that I have brought you home. She does not trust me.' He went into the living-room and picked up the phone. '*Allo, allo*, who is that?' After a moment he replaced the receiver with a shrug of puzzlement. '*Personne!*' he said. 'Nobody.'

Philippa took off the wrap she had borrowed from Chloe and made a pot of tea. 'It is the English way to finish an evening, drinking tea,' she teased Pascal when he pretended to pout because it wasn't coffee. They sat down and talked of their evening together, and Philippa told him warmly how much she had enjoyed herself and watched his pleasure.

At last, reluctantly, he got to his feet. 'Now I must leave you,' he said, 'or else I shall forget my promise to be very, very good. One small kiss—yes?'

He kissed her expertly and gently, and Philippa allowed herself to rest in his arms for a moment before she drew away. But the earth did not move beneath her, nor did stars explode over her head. 'Thank you for a lovely, lovely evening, Pascal,' she said. 'A perfect end to a perfect day.'

'For me too,' he said quietly, and left her rather quickly, with instructions about working the security lock and a promise to pick her up in the morning and drive her to the airport.

It was drizzling with rain as Philippa's taxi from Leamington Station drew up outside number sixteen Albany Square the following afternoon. The glow of the last two lovely days was fading fast. She tried to kindle a spark of optimism as she looked over the railings at the new presses in the printing shop below, but nothing happened. She was just tired, she told herself; it would be all right in the morning.

Mary was in her reception-office. She looked up from her desk with a welcoming smile as Philippa walked in. 'Hello again—had a nice time?'

'Marvellous!' A little of the magic of Paris surfaced again and Philippa's eyes were shining.

Then, from the inside office, Bart appeared, and there was no welcoming smile on *his* face. 'So you're back,' he said.

Philippa met the cold blue stare and shivered inwardly.

She was, she thought, back indeed!

CHAPTER TEN

IT WAS like a sauna bath—like being thrown out into the snow after all the love and warmth of the last two days. Philippa could feel herself freezing as she turned to go up to her flat.

'Just a moment.' Bart held up a hand. 'I'm on the point of leaving. Mary has a message for you, but I may as well tell you myself now you're here. I've arranged with John Pargeter for Friday. They'll be along about six and I'll come with them. We've discussed the details, haven't we, Mary?'

He directed a nice smile towards Mary, but snapped it off immediately as he turned back to Philippa. 'That's all, I think. I won't keep you now. I expect you're tired—after all your socialising. Goodnight.' He went out of the office.

Mary frowned. 'What was all that about?'

Philippa sank wearily into a chair. 'He's cross with me. He didn't want me to go away.'

'Oh—I see.' Mary's brown eyes were very perceptive and Philippa wondered what exactly she did see.

'I expect I'll survive.' Philippa tossed it all away with a wave of her hand. 'Put me in the picture, Mary.'

Mary gave her the news. The computers and drawing tables for the design office upstairs had already arrived, and some of the photographic equipment was due to be installed tomorrow. At Bart's request she had bought wine glasses and plates, and she would go into town on Friday morning and lay on a selection of snacks for the evening. Bart was bringing champagne to toast the new venture. 'It'll be quite a party,' she said. She glanced sideways at Philippa. 'But I expect you've had your fill of parties in Paris.'

There was no reason now why Mary shouldn't know about the wedding. 'Lots of parties,' Philippa said. 'I went over to Paris for my sister's wedding.'

'How lovely for you! A wedding! I'd like to hear all about it when you have time. I think Mr Marchant was rather mean to be cross about your going,' Mary said warmly.

Philippa made no comment. It was all getting rather foolishly complicated. Fortunately at that moment Portly strolled in and jumped up on her lap.

'He's missed you,' Mary said. 'He's hardly touched his food.'

Philippa scolded the cat gently and carried him upstairs, talking to him as he wrapped his soft black and white body around her legs, demanding food. It was a comfort not to be quite alone in the cold, empty flat.

Friday was March at its worst, cold and blustery. Mary's mother was unwell, so Philippa sent Mary off home early and went into town herself to buy goodies from the delicatessen. At half-past five she set them out on a side-table in the office, with the plates and glasses, and arranged a vase of daffodils on the desk, trying not to think about the time when Bart had sent her flowers. She adjusted the setting of the electric radiators, and when she was satisfied with everything she went upstairs to tidy herself, ignoring the butter-

flies fluttering in her stomach. This first meeting with
their new customers had got to be a success. She
mustn't let Bart down.

She changed into her pleated plum-coloured skirt
and a freshly clean white silk blouse, made up her
face carefully, with a smoky grey eye-shadow to match
her eyes, and the new pink lip-gloss she'd bought to
take with her to Paris. She brushed her dark feathery
cap of hair until it shone, slipped her mother's gold
loop earrings into her ears, and surveyed herself in
the wardrobe mirror. Yes, she looked reasonably like
an efficient young businesswoman. Bart wouldn't be
ashamed of her; she just had to be pleasant, and let
him do most of the talking.

She heard the front door open below and the sound
of voices in the hall, and she ran lightly down the
stairs.

Bart smiled at her and held up two bottles. 'Here
we are, Philippa, and we've brought the needful.' He
looked more approachable than he had done last time
she had seen him, but probably that was for the benefit of the visitors.

Philippa was only vaguely aware of John Pargeter—
a large grey-haired man with a friendly smile, but she
was very much aware of the woman beside him.

Madeleine Clark was tall and willowy and fair, and
very, very smart. She wore black—a tailored suit with
a short, cut-away coat and a pencil-slim skirt ending
above the knee. A huge elaborate brooch which had
an ethnic look was pinned to the lapel of her jacket,
and her dark gold hair was cropped short above the
ears. Her china-blue eyes moved appraisingly over
Philippa as Bart introduced them, and Philippa
wished she had chosen to wear anything rather than

the pleated plum-coloured skirt, which suddenly seemed hopelessly dowdy.

'Hello, Miss Price, I'm so glad to meet you at last. Bart has told me so much about you.' Ms Clark touched Philippa's hand briefly and turned to Bart. 'A fascinating old house, Bart. A Regency gem—I don't wonder you were taken with it. So vast and roomy!' She shivered delicately.

Bart laughed. 'OK, I get the message, Madeleine. We still have to install central heating.' He put one hand, holding a bottle, to her back, guiding her towards the office door. 'Come along into the office; you'll find that tolerably warm.'

John Pargeter was saying something to Philippa, which she didn't catch, as they followed into the office. The sight of Madeleine Clark had left her stunned. She represented so exactly the picture she had optimistically built up of herself—of a girl on the up and up in the business world. Cool, confident, perfectly groomed, entirely self-assured. This was the kind of woman she herself would have to deal with in her new managerial position. She quailed at the thought.

Bart put the bottles on the side-table and pulled out chairs for the visitors. 'First things first: we must drink to the new-look Albany Press.'

Philippa stationed herself near the table as he opened the first bottle of champagne. 'Very clever, my lad,' John Pargeter chuckled. 'Hardly a pop and not a drop spilled. I can't abide the modern fashion of spurting the stuff out like a fountain.'

Bart grinned, pouring out the champagne. 'I was instructed by a vintner in the Champagne district who had a proper respect for ritual and tradition.' He handed the glasses round and toasts were drunk. Philippa offered a dish of vol-au-vents to Ms Clark, who wriggled her small, perfect nose apologetically. 'Prawn? I'm so sorry—I'm afraid I'm allergic to prawns. No, don't worry—I'll just have a few nuts.'

Philippa turned for the tray of nuts and managed to catch the hand in which Ms Clark was holding her champagne glass. The glass tilted and a few drops of wine were spilled on Ms Clark's expensive black kid pumps.

'Oh, please—it's nothing at all.' Charmingly she checked Philippa's frantic search for a paper napkin, and turned to the two men, who were exchanging views on French wine districts.

The talk moved on to business matters. 'What did you think of the last book in our series, Bart—the one I posted to you?' John Pargeter enquired.

'Pretty good—but the next one will be even better,' Bart promised, with a smile. 'We've talked it over, haven't we, Madeleine?'

'Indeed we have, Bart.' The china-blue eyes held his meaningfully for a moment and then slid round to Philippa, who had been hovering in the background, saying nothing at all, and the eyes held an unmistakable message. 'I'm sure Miss Price will be looking forward to producing a super book—you have a diploma in design, of course, Miss Price?'

Philippa passed her tongue over dry lips as Bart cut in cheerfully, 'Philippa has a natural talent for art and design. Far more valuable than any scrap of paper. And do drop the "Miss Price", Madeleine. We're all friends here.'

'Of course,' cooed the girl. 'And I'm Madeleine. Now tell me what preliminary ideas you have for the artwork of our next book, Philippa. I thought myself that the typeface of the one we've just published wasn't altogether satisfactory. What alternative would you suggest?'

'Oh, I—I thought it was quite good,' Philippa managed lamely, feeling hopelessly out of her depth. To her, type was just type—tiny letters that she had often seen Ernie slotting into grooves in a wooden block.

Bart laughed again. 'Philippa is just being polite, Madeleine. Actually she suggested that we might do better with Gaudy Old Face for our first effort. We'll have to see, won't we?'

'Sounds OK to me,' John Pargeter said comfortably, helping himself to another sausage roll from the plate which Philippa hurried across the room to offer him—hoping that he wouldn't notice the deep flush of angry embarrassment that was rising into her cheeks. The woman was baiting her deliberately, making her look a fool in front of the two men. The fact that Bart was covering up for her only made it worse.

Madeleine nibbled delicately at a Brazil nut and sipped her champagne. 'Lovely!' she murmured, putting down her glass and seeking Bart's eyes again. 'Now, are you going to show us all your marvellous new equipment, Bart?'

Philippa trailed round after the other three as they went from room to room. She wasn't taking very much notice of the proceedings because she was immersed in her own dark thoughts.

As they were leaving the new design studio upstairs Madeleine leaned her blonde head towards Philippa.

'Have you a bathroom I could use? I left Birmingham in rather a hurry.' She smiled, sweetly apologetic.

'Of course,' Philippa said. She should have thought of this herself. Another black mark to her—to add to the rest. She led the way to the large family bathroom which had been redecorated for use by the studio staff.

Madeleine looked round admiringly. 'Everything's been so beautifully arranged,' she gushed. 'It will be such a pleasant place to visit. I always like to liaise with the printers of our books, so I'll be working closely with you...and with Bart, of course.' She smiled silkily. 'It's lucky that he and I get on so *very* well. We've been seeing quite a lot of each other lately.'

Philippa couldn't bear much more. Her stomach was aching with tension and her throat felt as if a great hard lump had lodged in it. 'Come down when you're ready,' she said, and went out of the room.

The round-tour ended in the hall. John Pargeter shook hands with Bart and Philippa. 'Very many thanks. It all looks extremely satisfactory. We'll certainly be glad to entrust you with our next opus, won't we, Madeleine?'

'Oh, indeed, I've just been telling Philippa how much I'm looking forward to it. I'm sure we'll all work together splendidly.' The china-blue gaze passed over Philippa and rested on Bart.

Then she seemed to think of a final trick that she had omitted. She smiled sweetly at Philippa. 'When our subs have finished with the copy I'll bring it along and we can work on the CRC together, can't we, Philippa?'

Philippa didn't say anything. It didn't really matter now that she hadn't the faintest idea what a CRC was.

John Pargeter said, 'I'm joining my wife in Knowle; she's visiting her mother there. I can drop you off on the way, Madeleine, if you like.'

'Thanks, John, but it's out of your way and Bart's promised to give me a lift.' She put a white hand possessively on Bart's arm as they moved towards the steps.

He turned back to Philippa. 'I'll be in touch tomorrow,' he said. 'We have a lot to discuss.'

Philippa stood at the top of the steps and watched the two cars drive away. It was bitterly cold and a strong wind was tossing the trees about in the square. But she hardly felt the cold—she felt numb and bruised, that was all. Perhaps it was true what they said—that when you were devoured by a man-eating tiger you didn't feel the pain.

She went in and closed the heavy front door. Then she cleared away the remains of the party in the office and swept the crumbs off the carpet. She carried the plates and glasses into the kitchen and washed them up. The old kitchen was one thing that hadn't yet been altered, although it was scheduled, later, to be part of the photographic department.

Everything was changing. It wasn't her home any longer, and it wasn't her business either. But that wouldn't have mattered if Bart had loved her. She bowed her head over the sink and turned the cold tap on hard, to drown her sobs.

Suddenly through all the misery, the certainty came that she didn't want to go on. Love didn't enter into Bart's calculations; he would never know how much she yearned for him to love her.

Tomorrow, when he phoned, she would ask him to see her and she'd explain that the partnership wouldn't go ahead. Probably he'd buy her out and run the whole thing himself. She wouldn't really be missed; Mary was quite capable of doing her job here; her own had never been any more than a glorified secretary's job, anyway, she told herself. Her fantasy of being an owner-manager seemed remote, ludicrous really.

She went up to the flat and made tea. The thought of food was nauseating. Outside, the wind was getting stronger; it howled and screeched round the tall old house as Philippa sat with Portly on her lap and looked unseeingly at an old black and white film on TV. At ten o'clock she turned out the light and went into the bedroom. Portly followed, jumped up on the bed and settled down. He seemed almost to know that she didn't want to be alone tonight.

Philippa lay down beside him and pulled the quilt over her. She'd undress later on.

The wind was howling like a banshee now. An extra-vicious gust set the sash-window rattling. Philippa debated whether it was worthwhile getting up to try to wedge it, but decided it wasn't. She lay back and listened to the whistling in the rafters. It was as if the world were coming to an end.

And perhaps her world was, she thought. Everything had gone wrong—everything. She had dreamed of restoring the Albany Press to a position of success and prestige all by herself, but that had been doomed from the start. She had dreamed of being a businesswoman—suave and self-assured like Madeleine Clark, but she had gone down without a fight at the first sign of aggression. She had fallen in love with Bart, but she'd been too scared to take what he offered and now it was too late. She was an utter, utter failure. Nothing but a wimp.

Portly gave a low growl. Philippa reached out and stroked his head. 'It's all right, darling, it's only the wind. Nothing to be afraid of.'

But Portly knew better. He wriggled from under her hand and landed with a soft thud on the carpet. Almost at the same moment there was a noise like a sonic boom as the gale hurled its full fury against the tall old house. An ominous cracking sounded from the attic above. Petrified, Philippa dragged herself up in the bed and at the same moment there was a shattering crash and all the lights went out. She covered her face with her hands to protect it from the sharp pieces of the ancient lath and plaster that began to fall from the ceiling. A thin, icy draught was blowing into the room from somewhere.

She must get out of here quickly—quickly. She slid off the bed, her legs shaking violently, and, in the total darkness, made for where she thought the door was. She walked straight into the dressing-table, struck her head against something sharp and collapsed on to the floor, dazed and whimpering, her mouth full of dried plaster.

She could hear nothing but the scream of the wind, feel nothing but the heavy thudding of her heart. And then she heard a voice from somewhere below. 'Philippa—Philippa—are you there—are you all right?'

It sounded like Bart's voice, but it couldn't be. Bart was miles away, tucked up cosily in bed with Madeleine Clark.

'Philippa!' The voice came nearer. The thin white beam of a torch shone on her face. 'Are you hurt, Philippa?'

'No—I don't think so,' she mumbled. 'I bumped into something and fell over.'

He shone the torch upwards. 'Looks as if a chimney's down—half the ceiling's gone. We'd better get out of here before anything worse happens. Let me help you.' His arms round her, they stumbled down the stairs together.

His car was standing outside the house. He opened the door and bundled her in, muttering under his breath. He was probably blaming her for not having the roof examined long ago.

'I'll take you home with me,' he said. 'You can have a bath and a bed for the night—you can't stay here.' The engine throbbed into life. He put his hand on the gear lever.

Philippa's mind seemed to go into reverse. 'Stop,' she screamed, over the roar of the wind. 'I've got to go back.' How could she have forgotten Portly?

'You're not going back in there; whatever you've left behind will have to stay there,' Bart rasped, and the car moved forward.

She clutched his arm. 'Stop—you've got to stop.' she yelled. 'I've left Portly in there and I've got to go back for him.'

He swore under his breath. 'He'll get out—cats have nine lives.' He put his foot down on the accelerator.

Philippa fumbled wildly with the door-handle.

'It's locked,' Bart said.

She tried to wind down the window. 'If he's killed I'll never forgive you,' she sobbed.

The car stopped, backed up to the pavement again. 'OK,' Bart said with infinite weariness. 'If your cat has to be got out then that's that.' He opened the car door and unclicked his seatbelt. 'And don't you dare move until I come back.'

There were no street lights, but the moon had risen. In the light that seeped through the scudding clouds Philippa saw Bart run up the steps, open the front door and disappear inside the house.

For a moment or two she sat rigid, petrified with fear. Then she heard a rumble, high up, and had a terrifying picture of Bart lying buried under a pile of rubble. She wriggled to the driving seat, opened the door and staggered up the steps after him.

The hall was in darkness, but she could make out the glimmer of a torch light, much higher up. She stumbled up the stairs, holding on to the banister, fighting for breath through the thick plaster dust hanging in the air. Up and up—she'd never known there were so many stairs. There was another rumbling sound from above and her heart gave a great lurch. For a moment she stopped, clinging to the banister rail.

Then the torch light turned a corner and Bart was there beside, her, Portly under his arm.

He swore violently. 'I told you to stay in the car. Go on—get down again—quickly.'

Somehow they were down in the hall again. Somehow she was sitting in the car, Portly on her lap, and she was weeping in a choky kind of way.

The rain had started now. It was lashing against the windscreen as Bart climbed in beside her. He hesitated for a moment and then leaned down to the small, crumpled figure in the corner of the passenger-seat.

'Why did you do that, Philippa? Why did you come after me?' His voice was surprisingly gentle. 'You were worried about the cat, was that it?'

She shook her head silently. 'About you,' she gulped, and added under her breath, 'because I love you.' But in the noise of the wind and the rain she didn't suppose he heard her.

Bart switched off the engine outside the cottage twenty minutes later. 'That's a relief; we're here, safe and sound. There's always the danger of fallen trees on a night like this. Are you asleep, Philippa?'

Not a word had been spoken on the drive. She had been sitting back with her eyes closed, holding Portly against her as he licked furiously at his fur, trying to remove the small shards and powdered plaster.

She sat up. 'Your housekeeper won't be pleased to see me—dropping plaster all over her beautiful floors.'

'Don't be silly,' Bart said shortly. 'Come along in. Anyway, Mrs McLeod isn't here—she's staying in Nuneaton with her sister overnight. Just as well perhaps,' he added obscurely.

He led her into the cottage, switching on lights as he went. 'Now, then,' he said briskly. 'You'd like to clean up. Come along upstairs—the spare room's all ready. We keep it ready for my parents. They're retired now and have a habit of dropping in unexpectedly. There's a shower-room attached, but if you'd rather have a good long soak in a bath I'll be pleased to lend you mine.'

He led the way upstairs—chatty, relaxed, dropping easily into the role of the perfect host. Philippa wondered painfully if he'd entertained Madeleine Clark here often, when he gave his housekeeper the night off.

The guest-room was warm and luxurious and very feminine. 'My mother keeps a selection of clothes here.' Bart gestured towards the built-in wardrobe. 'Help yourself—she won't mind in the least. The bathroom's second along the passage. I'll go down and see what Mrs McLeod's left for supper. And I'd better ring up the police in Leamington and alert them to what's happened. There may be danger to cars or pedestrians.' He nodded pleasantly to her and went out of the room.

Philippa was still hugging Portly. She put him down now and he started immediately on a tour of the room, inspecting every corner. When satisfied, he sat down at the foot of the big double bed and began to clean his coat again.

Philippa found a pink towelling bathrobe in the wardrobe. She slipped out of her dusty clothes and made a neat heap of them in a corner of the room. Then, with the bathrobe round her, she made her way to the bathroom.

It was heaven to soak in blissfully hot water in a spacious bathroom, after making do for years with the cramped little shower-room in her flat. As she lay there, gazing at the blue tiles on the ceiling, all the horrors of the evening drifted away. Bart was safe. Portly was safe. That was really all that mattered.

She was sitting at the dressing-table, wrapped in the pink robe, drying her hair with a fleecy blue towel, when Bart knocked at the door and came in.

She hadn't seen him wearing casual clothes before, and the sight of him, looking fabulous in grey trousers and open-necked sports shirt, his brown hair wet from his shower, set her heart racing.

'Everything OK?' he enquired cheerfully. 'There's rather a nice-looking chicken casserole ready to pop into the microwave when you feel like eating.'

He came further into the room and gently took the towel out of her hands. 'Or,' he added softly, glancing towards the bed, 'could it be that there are more important matters for us to attend to first?'

She stared up at him, her mouth falling open, an odd kind of cramp gripping her stomach. There was no misunderstanding his words.

He regarded her quizzically, blue eyes very dark. 'I wasn't mistaken? You did say you loved me, didn't you, my darling? So I just thought...'

She didn't have to think. She was on her feet in a second and hurling herself into his arms, the pink robe flying open. 'Oh, Bart—yes—yes,' she wept.

Her body, naked under the open robe, was soft and warm, and flushed from her bath. Bart held her against him and buried his face in her damp hair. 'Oh, my precious girl,' he groaned, 'I thought it was too late. I thought I'd lost you.'

He lifted her in his arms and carried her to the bed. She lay there gazing up into his rapt face as he leaned over her, and all the love she had been unable to express was in her eyes.

'Beautiful—you're beautiful, and I love you so much,' he muttered brokenly. Gently he lifted her to ease her arms out of the robe, and the touch of her skin seemed to inflame him. A moment later his clothes had joined the robe on the floor and he was lying beside her, resting on his elbows, still looking down at her as if he could never look enough.

Then his mouth met hers in a heart-stopping kiss that went on and on, drawing out the sweet essence of her, making her senses swim in anticipation. His mouth slid down to caress her nipple with his tongue and she arched against him convulsively, crying out his name over and over again. His hands moved over her body, searching out the erotic places, and his lips followed, until she was roused to a passion and need that made her beg for release. Only then did he roll over and cover her body with his, entering her with a sure thrust.

His possession of her was at first slow and gentle and more voluptuous than anything she had known or imagined. When it became more urgent she matched her rhythm to his, uttering little moans of delight, and as she rose higher and higher on a tide of ecstasy and tipped over the edge, crying out his name over and over, he found his own release, shuddering against her with a hoarse indrawn breath of satisfaction.

Slowly they came down from the heights, and lay, satiated and without any need for words, locked in each other's arms. After a time they both slept.

Philippa was the first to wake. The heavy weight of Bart's arm was thrown across her stomach, and one leg was entwined in hers as if he was yoking her to him, dominating her, possessing her. A soft, loving smile touched her mouth. All the things she had once vowed to escape! But this was quite, quite, different.

He stirred and opened his eyes, and she lifted herself and planted a kiss on his shoulder, where a small tuft of dark hair tickled her lips. 'I always thought we should have an affair,' she whispered, 'only I was so stupid about it.'

He smiled his lazy smile. 'This will be the shortest affair on record. We get married as soon as we can gather our families together and put my ring on your finger.'

'But Bart...' she struggled to sit up, and he pulled her down again ' ... you don't have to marry me. Not unless...' She broke off, her eyes widening.

'Unless...' he mocked her gently. 'We could start a family sooner rather than later. I'd like it sooner myself—would you mind?'

A little boy with Bart's blue eyes, Bart's thick dark hair, Bart's zest for life! 'I'd like that more than anything,' she murmured dreamily.

'Good,' he said, and then, drawing in an unsteady breath, 'shall we see if can make it happen, then? This time it will be better.'

'Couldn't be.' She shook her head.

'Bet you,' he laughed. Then he wasn't laughing any longer as she turned into his arms in perfect trust and love.

Some time after two o'clock in the morning they got up and heated Mrs McLeod's casserole in the microwave and carried it into the living-room. Outside, the wind still gusted intermittently and rain pattered against the window, but inside the cottage it was warm and cosy. Bart threw more logs on to the fire and they sat close together on the sofa, balancing their plates on their knees.

There was a lot of explaining to do. 'I never knew you had a sister in Paris,' Bart said.

'And I never knew you had a brother in Australia,' Philippa put in. 'We really don't know much about each other, do we?'

He said ruefully, 'And what we do know seems to be wide of the mark very often.' There was a silence and then he blurted out, 'I thought you'd gone out to that French fellow who was hanging round you in Leamington. I was nearly going out of my mind. I was in such a state by one o'clock in the morning that I couldn't stand it any longer, so I rang the Paris number you left.'

'Oh, it was you on the phone,' Philippa said. 'We'd just got in.'

'And I take it it was the same bloke who answered the phone. What's his stupid name?'

A dimple danced in her cheek. 'Pascal,' she said. 'He was sweet—after the wedding he took me to a nightclub.'

'And . . . ?' he growled dangerously.

'And kissed me goodnight very chastely. Before she left on her honeymoon Chloe had made him promise to look after me, and he behaved like a perfect gent. I slept alone—and very soundly.'

'And I didn't sleep at all,' he growled. 'You put me through it, I can tell you.'

She said sweetly, 'It was your own fault. You shouldn't have been so horrid to me about going, and then I would have explained. Anyway, I thought you had fallen for Madeleine Clark. She thought so too.'

He shook his head. 'Never in this world, believe me.' He was silent for a long time, staring into the fire. Then he said, 'Do you remember telling me that your business was the most important thing in your life?'

She said, 'It wasn't true. I was hurt—and disappointed. I thought you were going to—to proposition me, and I was sort of hoping you would. But all you wanted to talk about was saving my business.'

He said heavily, 'Paula said exactly those same words. She said, "My business is the most important thing in my life." The next day she walked out on me to a fellow who had promised to put a lot of cash into her boutique.' He reached for the poker and pushed a log further back into the fire.

After a silence he went on, 'That night after the theatre I knew I was falling in love with you, but I was scared. I couldn't take the risk of it all happening again. Can you understand?'

'I can understand very well,' Philippa said quietly. 'I was let down too. Some day I'll tell you about it, but not now.' She took both their plates, put them on the floor beside the sofa, and curled up close against Bart. He put an arm round her and it was wonderful to be safe, and loved, and wanted. Portly jumped down from the chair he'd already claimed as his own, and inspected the empty plates hopefully. Finding nothing of interest, he yawned and jumped back again.

Philippa said, 'How did you come to be there, outside the house, just when it all happened? It was like a miracle.'

'It was like a nightmare to me. When I heard the crash and knew you were up there I died a small death. Oh, my darling girl, I do love you so much, I can't believe...' His voice shook.

After a silence he went on more steadily, 'I went home after I'd dropped Madeleine off. But I couldn't settle. Things seemed to have gone so wrong between you and me. I wanted to have a chance to put them right. And I was worried about you in the storm, all alone. I thought you might be frightened.' He drew her even closer. 'So I came back. I must have driven round the block half a dozen times, to get up my courage. It had started to rain and the wind was getting alarming, so I decided to chance my luck. I was getting out of the car when I heard the crash. The rest you know.'

'I still think it was a miracle,' Philippa said. 'We *are* really here together, aren't we?'

He reached out and switched off the table-lamp. 'I'll prove it to you,' he said huskily, slipping the pink robe off her shoulder.

A long time later Philippa lifted her head from Bart's shoulder and said, 'I'd almost forgotten about the Albany Press. Will the workrooms be damaged, do you think?'

'I shouldn't think so. Probably the two top floors took most of the fall. The insurance should cover that. You won't be able to live in your flat, sweetheart. You'll have to come here and live with me.' He chuckled wickedly. 'Mrs McLeod will act as nominal chaperon—very nominal.'

Philippa sighed. 'What a one-track mind the man has! How do I get to the office?'

'Simple—you commute. I'll drop you off on my way to Birmingham.' He added thoughtfully, 'How do you feel about the business, my darling? Shall I make you a wedding present of my share and then it can be all yours as you wanted? So long as I still have my dear old vintage handpress to amuse myself with.'

She sat up and glared at him in the firelight. 'Bart Marchant! Don't you dare desert me. I can't possibly manage on my own and you know it. Why, I didn't even know what a CRC was, when your Ms Clark sprung it on me.'

Bart said firmly, 'She isn't my Ms Clark—never was and never will be. And she's not all that clever—she was just showing off.' He added, 'CRC is "camera-ready-copy", for your information.'

She sighed. 'I've got such a lot to learn, but it'll be fun.'

His hand found its way inside the pink robe. 'And I've got such a lot to teach you, which will be even more fun.'

She covered his wandering hand with her own and said with mock-severity, 'We'll manage the business together—until the family starts to arrive. Then we'll have to see. I think Mary could well take over my job for a while, she's very capable.'

He laughed delightedly. 'Spoken like a true executive, preparing for all eventualities!'

'And don't you dare tease me either,' she added indignantly.

He was still laughing. 'Before we go into any more detail about the future of the Albany Press, may I make a suggestion, Madam Chairman?'

He stood up and drew her to her feet beside him. Then he framed her face in his two hands before he bent down to kiss her, and Philippa's heart shook at the love and tenderness in his dark blue eyes. 'What suggestion?' she whispered.

'Let's go back to bed,' said Bart.

Following the success of WITH THIS RING and
TO HAVE AND TO HOLD, Harlequin brings you

JUST MARRIED

SANDRA CANFIELD
MURIEL JENSEN
ELISE TITLE
REBECCA WINTERS

just in time for the 1993 wedding season!

Written by four of Harlequin's most popular authors, this
four-story collection celebrates the joy, excitement and
adjustment that comes with being "just married."

You won't want to miss this spring tradition, whether
you're just married or not!

**AVAILABLE IN APRIL WHEREVER HARLEQUIN
BOOKS ARE SOLD**